CATHERINE MANN

Awaken to Danger

D0037127

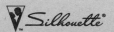

INTIMATE MOMENTS™

Published by Silhouette Books

America's Publisher of Contemporary Romance

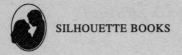 SILHOUETTE BOOKS

ISBN 0-373-27471-8

AWAKEN TO DANGER

Copyright © 2006 by Catherine Mann

This edition published by arrangement with Harlequin Books S.A.

® and TM are trademarks of Harlequin Books S.A., used under license.
Trademarks indicated with ® are registered in the United States Patent
and Trademark Office, the Canadian Trade Marks Office and in other
countries.

Visit Silhouette Books at www.eHarlequin.com

Printed in U.S.A.

Books by Catherine Mann

Silhouette Intimate Moments

Wedding at White Sands #1158
*Grayson's Surrender #1175
*Taking Cover #1187
*Under Siege #1198
The Cinderella Mission #1202
*Private Maneuvers #1226
*Strategic Engagement #1257
*Joint Forces #1293
*Explosive Alliance #1346
*The Captive's Return #1388
*Awaken to Danger #1401

Silhouette Bombshell

Pursued #18

Silhouette Books

Anything, Anywhere, Anytime

HQN Books

A Soldier's Christmas
"The Wingman's Angel"

*Wingmen Warriors

CATHERINE MANN

writes contemporary military romances, a natural fit,
since she's married to her very own USAF research
source. Prior to publication, Catherine graduated with a
B.A. in fine arts: theater from the College of Charleston,
and received her master's degree in theater from UNC
Greensboro. Now a RITA® Award winner, Catherine
finds following her aviator husband around the world
with four children, a beagle and a tabby in tow offers
her endless inspiration for new plots. Learn more about
her work, as well as her adventures in military life, by
visiting her Web site: catherinemann.com. Or contact her
at P.O. Box 41433, Dayton, OH 45441.

With deep admiration, I humbly dedicate this book to a real life "Scorch," who won his personal battle through an incredible strength of will and spirit. (You know who you are.) Many thanks for discussing your own recovery journey with me as I wrote this book.

"God grant me the serenity to accept the things I cannot change, courage to change the things I can and wisdom to know the difference."

("Serenity Prayer," made well-known through Alcoholics Anonymous by Reinhold Niebuhr who attributes the inspirational saying to Friedrich Oetinger.)

Chapter 1

Where was she, and where the hell were her clothes?

Flat on her back in a strange bed, Nikki Price stared up at the ceiling fan moving slower than the spinning ceiling. *Click, click, click.* Blades cycled overhead in the dim light, swaying the chain with a tiny wood pull dangling from the end.

"Ohmigod, ohmigod. *Oh. My. God.*" What had she done last night?

She tried to look around but her eyeballs seemed stuck, all swollen and gritty in their sockets, her head too heavy to lift off the fabric-softener-fresh pillow, sheets equally as soft against her bare skin. All over bare. Goose bumps prickled over her *completely* naked body.

"Not right," she whispered to herself, her quiet voice bouncing around the quieter room sporting a hotel-generic decor. "Not right, not right."

Her bedroom fan pull sported a miniature soccer ball with tiny flowers painted on the white patches, a gift from her brother last Christmas. "Okay, I'm not totally losing it if I'm noticing silly details like overhead fixtures, right?"

No one answered. Thank God.

Still, nothing was familiar in the dim bedroom, only a hint of early sunrise streaking through the blinds. Voices swelled outside the walls. Her stomach clenched.

Okay, almost definitely a hotel.

She inched her fingers under the covers across the mattress, farther, farther again. Empty. She searched her mind for clues before she would have to turn her head and confront whoever might be in the room with her.

Panic stilled her more than even the nauseating ache stabbing through her skull. She hadn't drunk much the night before. Had she? She scrolled through the evening, getting ready to go to Beachcombers Bar and Grill for the live music—and a neutral place to break things off with Gary. But she couldn't recall much of anything after asking for a second amaretto sour. She wasn't an angel, but she'd never expected to wake up in a strange bed.

Of course she hadn't expected to do a lot of the reckless things she'd done over the past seven months since Carson Hunt tromped her heart. Truly tromped. Not the sort of temporary hurt that came from having a crush go south or getting dumped by a guy she'd just met. No. He'd deep down damaged her soul so much that even thinking about him still made it difficult to breathe. The ache of betrayal by her first real love might never go away.

Although these days she was more mad than hurt.

Could she have been mad enough last night to do something beyond reckless? Something totally stupid. Apparently she had since here she was. She'd thought she was ready to break up with the latest loser she'd been dating in hopes of filling that empty spot left by Carson. Finally she would move on with her life.

Okay, so she dated Air Force pilots—like Carson. From the base where Carson was stationed. And most of them happened to be tall and blond like, well, *Carson*. It had only taken her seven months to make the connection—hello?—but once she had, she'd resolved to set her life right again and end things with her latest Carson substitute, Gary Owens.

No wonder she'd frozen up when any of those dates so much as kissed her. She wasn't interested in *them*. Which made her feel even worse. No guy—even a loser—deserved to be used as a replacement for another man.

Her stomach rebelled. So why was she naked in a hotel room? Apparently she'd gotten over her kissing aversion.

She swallowed down fear along with a prayer that whoever she'd been with had used a condom. From here on out, *she* would stop being such a loser. She risked a deeper breath, inhaling the scent of laundry detergent. Masculine cologne—ohmigod.

Breathe in.

Breathe out.

Breathe in…cologne and an air of something else, an unfamiliar smell she couldn't quite identify, but her body shivered in disgust all the same. Somebody was in the room with her. Still asleep? Or in the bathroom?

Please, please, please at least let it be Gary, even if they'd never slept together before. He hadn't been at the bar last night for those few minutes and couple of drinks she *could* remember, but he'd been the one to set up the meeting by sending her an e-mail asking her for a date.

Bracing herself for the worst anyway, she arched her aching body, her head pounding as she rolled onto her side under the cotton sheets. Fresh pain pounded as her cheek met the pillow, but she stifled the urge to moan. The room appeared as empty as the bed. She gulped in gasping breaths, her heart now hammering harder than her head, relief making her darn near dizzy. At least if he was in the bathroom, she would have a second to collect herself.

Palms flattened to the mattress, she angled up, cool morning air prickling along her skin. Winters in South Carolina were all the chillier for the humidity. Cold and damp, like the ancient tombs her junior high students were currently studying in honors history class—and ohmigod, she was going to be late for work.

"Hello?" Her voice crackled up her parched throat. "Uhm, I would really appreciate it if you wrapped a towel around yourself before coming out."

She didn't risk guessing a name.

Nikki waited, but still no sounds from the shower or anywhere else. She squinted to look through the dim morning light across the room. The tiny bathroom seemed abandoned. Relief rode a shuddering exhale racking through her.

She would worry later about the rest when she swiped the fog from her head. She wasn't off scot-free thanks to those unaccounted for hours, but she didn't have to confront the awful awkwardness—and horror—of facing some guy she couldn't even remember picking up.

New leaf turnover time.

Hell, she would turn over a whole flipping tree. She was done feeling sorry for herself just because Carson "Ultimate Loser" Hunt had drop-kicked her heart in one unforgettable night. She would take control of her life and her emotions.

Pressing the heel of her hand to her melon-heavy head, she swung her feet to the floor. *Thud.* Her toes struck something solid rather than carpet. She toppled forward, her heart double-timing to marathon pace.

Arms flailing she grabbed for the end table, slammed to her knees, her teeth jarring together. Pain sliced through her head. She squinted in the faint light….

And stared straight into the unblinking eyes of the dead man on the floor.

Major Carson "Scorch" Hunt was dead tired and he hadn't even eaten breakfast yet.

Of course he hadn't fallen into bed until two in the morning due to an emergency on the flight line and he was back at his desk by dawn, hoping for a more peaceful day. No such luck.

Now thanks to a phone call from the security police, peace was on hold for far longer than the sausage-and-egg croissant he'd picked up at a fast-food joint. On his way out the office door again, he jammed his arms back into his leather flight jacket that had never made it onto the brass anchor peg before his phone rang.

A lieutenant from his squadron was dead.

Damn it. His fisted hand snagged inside the sleeve. He punched it through.

He'd braced himself for the possibility of losing someone in battle, but not at home. Worse yet, the young pilot was Carson's responsibility as second in charge, since the commander was deployed to the Middle East with the other half of the squadron.

Shrugging the jacket over his shoulders, he bolted down the hall, through the glass door and out into the parking lot. Early-morning traffic clogged the base streets, adhering to the so-damn-slow speed limits. Screw it. The VOQ—visiting officer's quarters—was only about a mile away. On foot would be faster, taking him there in under five minutes. He sprinted through the web of parked cars, tucked through the creeping traffic, ignored the honks.

The phone call from base security police hadn't said more than Lieutenant Gary Owens was found dead in the VOQ with a woman.

Owens had an apartment downtown, but sometimes guys checked into one of the rooms for the night if they were partying nearby and too drunk to drive home—or if they lucked into unexpected plans for the night. *With a woman.*

Boots pounding pavement, Carson tried to block thoughts of exactly *which* woman Owens had been dating for the past month. Of course stemming thoughts of Nikki Price had been damn near impossible for a long time. For over two years, actually, since a pool party at a squadron member's apartment when he'd realized his crew member's daughter had grown up. Really grown up. Smart, sexy, twelve years his junior and the daughter of a man he respected and admired. Not to mention Carson wasn't in a place to offer any woman a secure, stable happily-ever-after.

And still he had weakened and betrayed his friend by sleeping with Nikki. Once. A mistake he couldn't repeat even though his pulse rate jackhammered through him at the mere possibility Nikki could be in trouble.

Carson left the road for a shortcut across the lawn, past pine trees and bare-limbed oaks. He had no claim to Nikki, and yet here he was, running like hell for her as much as the dead lieutenant. Her boyfriend.

He couldn't stomach thinking about her with Owens. But who else could be in that room? And if the guy had been cheating on Nikki with another woman then somebody deserved an ass kicking.

Except damn, damn, damn it all, Owens was already dead, a screwed-up kid who'd just gotten his life back on track. Carson had been so sure he'd helped the baby pilot, but had he intervened soon enough?

Think. Focus. If Nikki was inside that brick building, then she needed him, even if he was the last person she would want to see.

Each huffing bootstep drawing him closer, Carson trained his eyes on the security cop cars—at least a dozen—encircling the three-story building along with an ambulance. Looked like everyone who wasn't guarding the gates had been called. Police in camo and blue berets secured the scene. An SP—security police officer—guarding the front entry held up a hand.

Before the military cop could speak, Carson nodded. "I'm Lieutenant Owens's commander."

The SP nodded and saluted. "I'll radio ahead and let them know you're on your way, sir. Down that hall and around the corner."

"Thank you, Sergeant." Carson slowed his feet, if not his pulse that still slugged from dread more than the mile sprint.

He cleared the front desk and strode down the narrow carpeted hallway, taking the corner on a sharp pivot. The corridor hummed with organized pandemonium, more cops and base medical personnel, a couple of agents from the Air Force OSI—Office of Special Investigation.

His eyes scanned past to home in on one person.

A woman sat huddled in a chair outside a VOQ room, blanket wrapped around her while her teeth chattered, security cops on either side. He didn't need to see a face to recognize *her*. Nikki Price.

Hell.

She looked up, the motion jerky from shock most likely. Her eyes locked on his down the length of the passageway, dark circles underneath. Hair even darker tangled around her head in a silky mess that begged his fingers to comb through, to rest on her shoulders and pull her to his chest for the comfort she no doubt needed.

Her fingers went slack around the deep red blanket until the edge slid open to reveal her clothes. Jeans and a silky pink shirt, misbuttoned as if hastily snatched up and on—the same clothes she'd been wearing when he ran into her the night before. He stuffed back the kick of jealousy and moved closer. Still she didn't speak, a slight tightening of her full lips the only indication she registered his approach.

He wrestled with the detachment he would need to get through the next hour, a difficult battle. He looked past her into the room to the sheet over a body on the floor. Closing his eyes, he swallowed and winged a quick prayer for the dead man. There was nothing more he could do for Owens.

Nikki needed him.

Carson knelt beside her, too aware of the cops standing guard a few feet away. "Nikki?"

Finally, he let himself look at her face again even as he steeled himself for the unshakable draw combined with guilt that made it tough to think around her, much less speak. He worked to read her expression, but her face was blank. Still he couldn't miss the pale cast under her olive complexion.

She glanced up, frowning, confused. Or disoriented? Her shaky hand rose toward his face. "Your mustache. It's gone."

What an odd thing to notice, but then she had reason to be in shock. Her wounded eyes seemed so much older than her twenty-three years right now, a dangerous thought for him to have since their twelve-year age difference helped him keep his distance.

He stroked his freshly bare upper lip. "That's what I get for shaving on the fly when I was running late." Because his few hours at home during the night had been filled with thoughts of running into Nikki outside Beachcombers on her way in to meet up with another man. "What happened here?"

She shrugged, the blanket slipping farther. "Gary is dead." Her voice was low, overly calm but thready, a thin substitute for her normally husky and—God help him—sultry tones. "You probably already know that."

"How?"

"We're not sure. Sometime during the night he hit his head."

Hit his head? Drunk and stumbling around in the room? Possible. Yet something was still… off. "I'm sorry this had to happen to you. What can I do to help? Tell me and I'll do my damnedest to make it happen."

"Gary's the one we should be sorry for." Her fingers twisted in the burgundy blanket even as her face stayed composed. "Thank you for coming over, but the SPs have everything under control."

So why were they keeping her around?

God, he wished she were anywhere else right now. She should be on her way to work. She often went in early or on Saturdays to tutor at-risk students from other classes and schools. He shouldn't know so much about her, but his ears always tuned in when her father bragged about his daughter's graduation from college, her junior high teaching job, her latest marathon race.

Damn. He was a freaking sap when it came to this woman. Always had been.

Tearing his eyes away from her before he did something dumb like scoop her up and take her away, he stared at the shrouded body being hefted onto a gurney. "Owens was in my squadron. I have to be here for him, and your father would want me to look out for you."

Her father, a cargo plane loadmaster, was deployed to the Middle East. The last thing the Price family needed was more stress with J.T. in a war zone and his wife taking care of a toddler with another late-in-life baby on the way.

"I *am* okay." Nikki's teeth chattered faster in contradiction to her seeming composure.

"Right. And you're not in shock, either. Uh-huh." Carson shrugged off his jacket. No way did he want to think of her father right now or all that guilt would drive him to his knees.

He'd betrayed the man in the worst possible way, a man who was more than a friend, more than a comrade in arms. They'd been POWs together, the strongest of bonds.

He owed J. T. Price better than screwing the man's daughter. He couldn't make up for the past, but he could take care of the present by hauling Nikki out of whatever mess she'd landed her most excellent ass in.

Carson passed his jacket to her. She stared at the coat so long he wondered if she might simply ignore his offer. Finally, she took it from him carefully, without touching his hand.

The blanket slid around her waist as she shoved one arm then the other into his coat, a final shiver rattling her teeth. "I'm sure my dad will be grateful."

Not hardly.

He wanted to tell her he'd come for her, too, but that wouldn't be wise with a cop within earshot.

The gurney wheeled past with the sheet covering the outline of a body. She went even paler under her deep tan. She tanned easily thanks to her mother's Greek heritage—and what an inane thought in the middle of hell. "You still haven't told me what happened? How did he hit his head?"

Maybe he should pull the SP aside and speak with him instead, but he couldn't bring himself to leave her sitting alone.

"I don't know. I had a couple of drinks over at Beachcombers. I was nervous about—"

Please don't let her say she was nervous about sleeping with Owens.

"—about breaking up with him."

Thank God.

Or maybe not because that gave them all the more reason to have fought.

"I don't remember anything after the second drink. I can't even recall leaving Beachcombers, just waking up here."

Nikki didn't remember? Or was too embarrassed to say? Either way, he could tell now wasn't the time to push her.

He could see the fear in her wide eyes. Her foggy eyes? Something wasn't right. Her dilated pupils stared back at him in spite of the early-morning sun through the windows and overhead light flooding the hall. Nikki didn't use drugs. He would bet his life on that.

Except no one ever believed his wealthy uptight parents were users, much less addicts, until his tenth grade English teacher. She hadn't been able to get the administration to do crap for him since his parents were six-figure contributors to the private school, but she'd pointed him toward Alateen. His parents weren't alcoholics, but the counseling principles had still applied for the child of addicts.

His teacher had also steered his parents toward enrolling him in a military prep school for his junior and senior years. A school far-the-hell away from his neglectful, abusive home life.

If Nikki had a problem, she needed help from someone better than him with his own secrets and demons.

"Maybe I should call your mother." He reached inside his thigh pocket for his cell phone. Nikki's mother, Rena, was also a counselor, even if she was on maternity leave.

"No!" She gripped his wrist with quiet desperation. Her slender fingers seared through his uniform sleeve. "Please. Mom has enough on her plate right now with Dad deployed, not to mention being over forty and pregnant again. She hasn't wanted people to know, but she's having a tough time with nausea, even a false labor scare. Please, don't call her. Okay?"

"You shouldn't be alone. Is there a friend I could call for you?"

She shook her head, tangled hair brushing her shoulders. "I don't want *anyone* to know, not yet at least."

"All right, but that means you're stuck with me." He shoved to his feet by the SP. "Have you finished questioning her?"

"For now. The lead OSI agent said he has more questions for later."

Carson glanced back into the room where two men in suits were crawling around the floor looking under the bed. The OSI was made up of part civilian investigators, part active duty military. Since the incident had happened on base, involving a service member, civilian police wouldn't even be involved. Would that be better or worse for Nikki? Who the hell knew anything right now except he had to get her out of here. "Then I'll take her home."

The cop stepped closer to Nikki's chair. "I'm afraid we can't let you do that, sir. She has to be checked out by a doctor first."

Doctor? They'd said *Owens* was the one who hit his head. Had something happened to her, too? That would account for the pupils and the confusion over what happened. "A doctor?"

He reached to brush back her hair for a better look at her face. She jerked away, flinching. From him or pain? Either way her hair swished to reveal a bruise on her cheek. What the hell had Owens done to her?

Scenarios he hadn't wanted to consider blared through his

head. He'd assumed Owens died in a freak accident—slipped in the bathroom or tripped over his pants or rolled out of bed. Carson pinched between his eyebrows. He didn't want that image of Owens in bed with Nikki. But the image of Owens hurting Nikki…

Hell.

Rage threatened to blind him. He blinked the red haze clear enough to function.

He scoured her clothes as if somehow he could develop Superman X-ray vision and find marks on her skin. No such luck, a curse and a blessing. But he did find other details he'd overlooked earlier—missing buttons on her silky shirt tugged on over a tank top. One of the knees of her jeans seemed more threadbare than the other, as if she'd skidded recently. He would wager money he would find a bruise beneath the denim.

There'd been an attack. A struggle. And somehow Owens had died.

"Nikki, did he hurt you?" Or worse. He blinked back the red fog again.

"I told you, I don't remember." Pride and a paper-thin bravado braced her shoulders. "Even if I did, this isn't your business or problem."

"Are you sure you don't want me to call your mother? She's going to find out eventually."

"And maybe we'll have a few more answers by then. I would like to get through—" she sucked in two shaky breaths "—the doctor's exam first."

She might not want his help, but he wasn't leaving her alone. He would protect her until she could take care of herself again.

He turned back to the SP. "She needs to leave. Now. Can't you see she's about to pass out? Who the hell knows what happened here but it's clear she was assaulted and needs treatment."

"Major, we're just doing our job and the investigator still needs to question her."

"He can do that at the hospital." He let all his anger seep steel into his words. "If she's been abused in any way and you've kept a traumatized woman sitting here alone—"

"We're moving things along as quickly as we can, Major, without compromising the crime scene."

"Is she being detained?"

"No, sir."

"Then she's ready to leave for the E.R." He slid an arm around her shoulders and eased her to her feet trying not to remember the last time he'd touched her this way or how many times he'd been tempted to put his hands on her body again.

His only defense had been distance. And now it looked as if he wouldn't be leaving her side anytime soon.

Chapter 2

Nikki tugged a surgical scrub shirt over her head and stifled a wince at the lack of underwear since all her clothes had been bagged for evidence. As if she didn't already feel exposed enough today.

At least the E.R. held more answers for her than her still-foggy head. She'd pulled it together enough during the police escort over to call in sick at school. Truth be told, she did feel sick, heartsick and body sore.

Paper crackled under her as she gingerly slid off the gurney, her toes hitting cold tile. Not as much of a shock as it could have been since she already felt chilled to her soul.

Bracing a hand on the cabinet full of gauzes, tongue depressors and latex gloves, she tugged on the surgical pants and knotted the tie before sliding her feet into the flimsy hospital slippers the nurse had given her. For the first time in her life she was grateful she could go braless. She could have sent Carson to her place to pick something up, but he wouldn't leave the hospital and she really didn't want him rooting through her underwear drawer.

What a silly thought. Except her brain seemed to hitch on the oddest details as if to fill empty space left by missing memories. At least the doctor reassured her it didn't appear that she'd had sex or been raped. She shuddered.

Any bruising stayed confined to her arms and ribs and Gary had been wearing his pants—even if they'd been around his ankles. All signs indicated if she'd killed him, she'd done so before penetration.

Her stomach cramped at the thought she could have taken a life, even in self-defense. She couldn't live with having killed someone, anyone, and to have known that person... Would she spend the rest of her life wondering what she could have done differently?

Or worse yet, never know.

Had she struggled and thrown him off? Or hit him with something? She was strong enough to do it after years of training on her university soccer team. She squeezed her eyes shut tight against tears so close to the surface, as if maybe she could find the memories from the night before glistening behind her eyes.

But nothing.

The shrink the E.R. had sent down for a consultation couldn't offer definitive answers, but he did say the memories could trickle back once her mind had a chance to adjust to the trauma of what happened.

Distraction. She needed a distraction and normalcy. She

snagged her cell phone from the rolling tray and settled into a steel-back chair rather than the exam gurney that held too many invasive memories. The message symbol flashed on the LCD screen. No surprise. She clicked through the numbers. Two from friends and then her mother's number—four times. She wouldn't be able to hold her off much longer and she certainly didn't want her mom to panic.

She would never be able to forgive herself if her mother lost the baby because of stress Nikki rained on her family's already overloaded life. A call should buy her a little time at least. She retrieved the stored number and waited—for only a ring and a half.

"Mom, hi, it's me. What's up?"

"Nikki Janine Price, you were starting to worry me." Her mother's voice held more concern than rebuke. "Are you all right? Where are you?"

Uh-oh. She recognized that tone well. Mom already knew the answer, or at least part of it.

But she wasn't a sixteen-year-old trying to hide a C on her report card. "I'm obviously not at work."

A benign response until she figured out how much her mother already knew. She'd learned a lot about finagling words after listening to her young students try to play her.

"I know that much. I called the school to leave a message for you and they said you're home sick today. You sound stuffy."

Duh. Because she'd cried her eyes out all over a nurse about an hour ago. At least her mom didn't seem to know about Gary Owens's death yet. "I'm just a little congested, nothing a steamy shower and a nap won't fix."

Liar.

She'd held strong all morning only to lose it when the doc put her in the stirrups. God, she'd gritted her teeth through pap smears before—bleck, nobody liked those after all—but she'd already felt so exposed, violated and outright scared to death. Tears were so darn embarrassing, even though the doc had patted her knee and said to take her time while the nurse passed Kleenex and comfort. Their sensitivity only served to make extra tears well up even remembering it now.

Her emotions were so fuzzy and out of control—like standing in a batting cage with one of those baseball pitching machines, and her reflexes too muddled to keep up with everything pelting toward her. All the more reason to stay away from her mom for a couple more hours.

She would go to her mother's house this afternoon and tell her in person before the rumor mill kicked in around base. Although the fallout in the press could be limited because of the exclusively military investigation.

"You didn't pick up at home, either. Are you at the doctor's?"

Mom radar. Its accuracy was scary. "Yes, I've seen a doctor." True enough. "Why did you call in the first place?" A new fear slithered through her hazy brain. "Are *you* okay?"

"I'm fine. Everything's wonderful in fact." Her mother's happiness darn near vibrated through the phone lines. "I had an ultrasound this morning and, well..."

The reason for her mother's call. Of course. "You wanted to share the excitement of the moment with someone since Dad couldn't be there."

"Pretty much, and who better to share it with than my daughter?"

Nikki pulled her tattered nerves together enough to speak

a while longer, for her mom, for her dad, too. "Everything looks good?"

"Perfect so far for a forty-two-year-old mother-to-be. I just need to keep my feet up after the spotting and cramping scare." She laughed low. "Am I crazy to do this?"

"You and Dad are great parents." They'd just sucked at being married for the first twenty-two years. Now that they'd finally figured it out, they seemed determined to start over in every sense of the word, including with a new pair of kids since their first daughter and son were already grown.

She admired her mother's determination, even as she resolved not to put herself through the hell of waiting for years for a man to get his head out of his butt and commit emotionally. "Could the technician see if it's a boy or girl?"

"Yes," Rena paused, "but I want to tell your father first."

"You know how I hate secrets." Her parents had tiptoed around telling their kids the truth about their problems, as if she and her brother Chris couldn't hear the fights and feel the dark silences afterward. She and Chris had kept their schedules packed as teenagers trying to avoid the tension.

"You'll be the first to know after I get in touch with him."

Nikki scrubbed a hand over her eyes. The dizziness kicked into overdrive, exhaustion nailing her. "I'm glad everything's cool with Freckle. I'll be looking forward to seeing the pictures later today. Okay?"

"Are you sure you don't need—"

"I just want a nap, then I'll come by later this afternoon. I promise." She swallowed hard. "I love you, Mom."

She disconnected, already dreading the conversation to come and the burden she would place on her family because of whatever the hell she'd done last night, because of her poor judgment in choosing Gary Owens. Her father was flying in a hot zone and so didn't need the distraction of worrying about her. Although there was nothing she could do to stem the eventual tide of gossip that would flow through e-mail overseas.

Being an adult and independent meant accepting responsibility. What she did affected others—like her family.

Turning her back on her too-pale reflection in the medicine cabinet glass, Nikki scooped a rubber band from a rolling table and gathered her hair away from her face. She needed to get her life together and work on putting this behind her. No more nursing a ridiculous broken heart for a man who flat-out didn't care. She wouldn't be like her mother, losing years of her life waiting for a guy to realize what he was throwing away.

Besides, she had bigger concerns right now. Like getting through the interview with the OSI agent due to walk in the exam room.

Why wouldn't Nikki call a lawyer?

Thumbing the disconnect button on his cell phone call from work, Carson kept his eyes locked on the exam room door while he paced past the row of vinyl-covered chairs and sofas. If only he could infuse his will through the panel into the idealistic woman on the other side.

Growing up, he'd watched countless guilty-as-hell people get off with a slap on the wrist because of expensive counsel, greased palms and a few wealthy connections. How could she simply trust her entire future would be okay if she just told the truth? What little she could remember. He couldn't stomach even the possibility of Nikki losing her freedom when he knew without question that woman was *not* a murderer.

He'd spent the past couple of hours on the phone taking care of crises at the squadron, arranging for an officer, chaplain and doctor from a base near Owens's parents in Nebraska to make a notification visit. He wished the couple lived closer so he could have made the visit himself. But he would travel from Charleston to Omaha to attend the funeral, along with every squadron member available. Regardless of what Owens had done last night, he'd still been an officer under Carson's command.

The door swung open. The OSI agent ambled out, slow, but Carson wasn't fooled by the guy's sleepy-eyed act. Special Agent David Reis's cynical eyes were taking everything in, and Carson wasn't so sure cynicism would work in Nikki's favor.

Nikki stepped through a few paces behind the agent, speaking with the nurse at her elbow flipping pages on a metal clipboard, stray words drifting about lab results and release forms for her to sign. She seemed okay, steady on her feet and confident even in surgical scrubs that somehow managed to accentuate her mile-long legs and skim over gentle curves he had no business noticing, especially today.

Good God, regardless of how strong she looked, bruises still marked her arms and heaven only knew where else. He forced his hands not to clench. He kept tracking her moves, searching for answers—or at least clues—as to what happened when the uneasiness settled with the weight of a stare boring into him. Slowly, Carson turned.

Special Agent Reis stared back with those half-open assessing eyes.

Carson nodded toward Nikki. "She's free to go?"

"Yes, sir, as soon as she finishes signing her release papers. We've covered everything for now. She just needs to stay in town until we have a few more answers." Absently, Reis reached into his inside jacket pocket, frowned then brought his hand back empty. "You're going to take her home?"

"Yes."

"Good." He fished into his pants pocket and brought out gum this time. "No matter what shook down in that VOQ room, she's had a helluva shock."

Carson tugged his leather jacket off the back of a waiting room chair. "Guess you can't tell me what she said."

"You'd guess right." He folded a piece of gum into his mouth. "Sorry."

"You're only doing your job." He understood all about that. He wouldn't get anything more out of the detective, but it wouldn't hurt to be amiable and form a connection that might lead the guy to give him a heads-up about info in the future. Carson nodded to the empty gum wrapper in Reis's hand. "Just quit smoking?"

Reis grin-grimaced. "Yeah, I still reach for the cigarettes. Doublemint sticks aren't helping much."

"Try drinking everything with a straw for a while."

"Like a drag from a smoke." His working jaw slowed. "Good call. Addictions suck."

"That they do." And since the opening was there, he continued, "Speaking of addictions, you need to know that Owens had a gambling problem. He seemed to have it under control, but…"

"Sometimes old contacts can still be hard to shake."

Nodding, Carson reached to stroke his mustache—damn it—only to find it gone. "I just thought you should know."

More than that he couldn't say without betraying confidences, and he really didn't know more that would be helpful. Still, he'd stuck to the standard squadron knowledge. Reis would have found out eventually. Carson had only sped up the process for safety's sake.

Reis studied him through half-open eyes. "Not that you have any reason to send me in a direction other than Nikki Price."

"I just thought you should know," he repeated.

"Duly noted." Reis tucked his gum pack back in his pocket and pivoted away.

Carson chewed on a curse harder than the investigator chomped gum. So much for keeping his damned drooling over Nikki a secret.

He could deal with the rest of the world knowing. But it was far tougher—and more essential—to keep the rogue attraction hidden from Nikki.

Rohypnol, a date-rape drug, had somehow been slipped into her drink last night.

Nikki settled into the bucket seat of Carson's sparkling Ford F-250, still rocked to her toes by the lab results that had arrived while Special Agent Reis questioned her. She hadn't been able to determine from the detective's expression if the news worked in her favor or not. Worst of all, there was less chance of her remembering now since the memory loss wasn't simply a by-product of trauma-induced stress.

A long sigh swelled low in her chest, rolling up without any real release in the tension kinking her muscles. The drizzly day outside Carson's windshield and pattering on the cab roof mirrored her mood. Thank goodness she wouldn't have to hold it together much longer. Another twenty minutes and she would be in her apartment.

Riding home with Carson was preferable to her trip over in the ambulance with Special Agent Reis. Barely.

Except she owed Carson big for the hours he'd spent looking out for her today so she wouldn't have to upset her mother. Sure he'd done it for her father, but he had seemed concerned for her, too…

God, she was already weakening around him again, the warmth and scent of his leather jacket more enticing than it should be. And while she'd always found his mustache sexy, his fully-revealed sensual upper lip was all the more enticing.

A dangerous thought.

Still, she should answer the unspoken questions lurking in the clammy air between them. "The doctor said I wasn't raped."

His knuckles went white on the steering wheel, even as his face stayed blank, aviator sunglasses hooked on the collar of his flight suit. "You didn't have to tell me, but thank you."

"Of course I would tell you." She scavenged a smile. "And you would have found out all the details anyway since you're Gary's commander."

He kept his eyes forward on the traffic-packed road, watching the streetlight. "I would have found out because I'm worried about you."

She let herself soak in the concern in his voice until the light turned green.

"Thank you." She blinked against the glare streaking through the window as the sun peeked from behind the clouds.

Her head thunked back to rest and she watched the telephone poles whiz past as they drove toward the winding bridge. Everything blurred from exhaustion and more. Definitely more than she wanted to acknowledge because then she would have to admit that spending time with Carson was important. "The hospital put a rush on my lab work. Someone slipped Rohypnol in my drink last night."

His curse hissed long and low. "And somebody's going to pay for that, no damn question."

"At least I understand the memory loss." Although that piece of knowledge came with another sense of having been violated. Who'd done it? She'd finished one drink before Gary arrived, and been almost through the second when he slid up beside her, elbow on the bar smiling as if totally unaware that their relationship was going nowhere. How could he have not realized?

Or had he? "I should be relieved I'm not suffering some mental break from trauma, right? Instead I'm just…"

"Pissed off. Of course you are." He glanced over at her, gray eyes steely with a repressed anger glinting through. "You have every reason to be upset."

Damn it, he'd given up the right to be her friend a long time ago. "Please quit being so nice."

"You want me to be an ass?"

She cranked the heater higher even though she knew the chill went bone deep from things that had nothing to do with dreary January weather. "I'd like an excuse to holler."

"I could take you out on my boat to the middle of Charleston harbor and let you yell if you think it would help."

"It won't."

"Are you sure you don't want me to call your mother?"

"No. I'll tell her. Later though—" She stopped short as an awful possibility pushed through her muzzy mind. "Do you think what happened will hit the news soon?"

"The basics, but the names are being withheld until Owens's family is notified."

She squeezed her eyes shut, guilt pressing hard against her chest over the crushing pain Gary's parents would suffer. Because of her?

"The investigator is withholding your name for your own safety."

What? She shifted in her seat to face him. "I thought they believed I'm guilty."

"They saw the wisdom of at least considering other options."

"Thank you."

"I didn't do anything."

"Thank you anyway for staying with me today."

"Your father would have my ass if I didn't look out for you. Sharing an enemy prison cell forges a bond I can't explain."

Those days when her father's crew had been missing, then reported taken by enemy warlords, had been hellish. She'd feared for her father's safety as well as for the man she'd thought she loved—even if at that time Carson had not noticed her beyond a kid sister kind of way.

Until later.

She so didn't need to think of later right now with him sitting so close and her in need of comfort in a big way. Who wouldn't be rocked by what had happened? But she was strong. She could hold on until she got in her apartment where she would have a long soggy cry in her bathtub. A man was dead, a man she'd cared about enough to date. A man she'd kissed and apparently nothing more, thank heavens, but he deserved to be mourned. Even if he'd done something so horrible she'd struck out and killed him.

Bashed in his skull.

Bile burned high in her throat. "Pull over."

"What?"

"Pull over or you're gonna need your carpet cleaned."

He whipped the truck across two lanes and onto the shoulder. She jerked her seat belt free and lurched from the cab to the swaying reeds and tall marsh grass.

Thank God he didn't join her while she heaved up her empty guts. If only she could pitch the horror of the day into the marsh grass, as well.

Finally, she straightened again, weaving as she sucked in chilly winter air until the double vision of afternoon traffic meshed into a single world again. Turning back, she found Carson leaning against the passenger-side door, waiting in case she needed him, but not intruding.

Emerging sunlight glinted off his blond hair and sunglasses now shielding his eyes, his body every bit as tall and strong and appealing as the first time she'd seen him strutting across a tarmac when she'd been waiting to welcome her dad home from an overseas tour. She was too tired and heartsore to feel attraction, but God, how she yearned to rest her head on that broad chest.

Instead, she planted her feet into the grassy incline and made her way back up slower than she'd descended.

She stopped beside him. Traffic whooshed past in blasts of wind.

Carson passed her a handkerchief without speaking. She took the small folded linen from his hand, three tiny initials embroidered in the upper corner. She studied the larger "H" with a "C" and "A" on either side. Who carried monogrammed handkerchiefs anymore? Apparently Carson. She'd thought he was a friend, had even shared a bed with him and didn't even know he carried a handkerchief, much less what the "A" stood for.

Nikki swiped the cloth across her mouth before clutching it in her fist. "Thanks."

"Are you all right now?"

"Who would be?"

"Right answer." His curt nod gave away less than his shielded eyes as he stood in the freezing mist without the least shiver. Maybe he seemed so perfect because he wasn't even human. "It'll take the drugs a while to wear off."

She sagged to rest beside him against the truck, drags of the prickly cold clearing her head. "So I didn't hurl because I'm an emotional wreck after all?"

"Over in Rubistan, after your dad and I were rescued, I barely made it to the barracks bathroom before I lost the MRE the soldiers gave me."

She pressed her fingers between her eyes against the ache his image brought. She'd hurt for him then and wasn't anywhere near as distant as she wanted to be now. "I appreciate your telling me that, especially since it must be difficult for you to talk about that time. My dad still doesn't discuss what happened over there very much."

Carson shrugged it off his broad shoulders as if it were no big deal when they both had to know otherwise. "We handle crap like that in different ways. The important thing is that you deal with it."

"Even if that means hurling in a ditch."

"Hey, join the trauma-hurling club." The strengthening sun glinted off his smile as brightly as it did his golden hair.

"And you're a badass." A badass who happened to look like an angel who could lead a saint to sin.

"So are you."

Ohmigod, everything had been easier when she could keep her distance from him. She could almost delude herself into thinking he wasn't as—charming?—no, that wasn't quite right. Carson had seemed nice, a flat-out nice guy she'd liked, admired, wanted so much she'd been a blind idiot.

She really needed to go home fast. "Thanks for the quick reflexes in pulling over. I'm ready to leave now."

"Are you sure you'll be okay alone?"

"You can't be offering to stay with me?" She knew full well he had to get back to the squadron. Already he would have to work late into the night to clear through all the work and crises that would have piled up while he was out of the office—

Whoa. Stop.

Why had she taken so much note of his work schedule when she'd been dating other guys? It had been bad enough before when she took note of everything about him, back when she'd thought he felt the same attraction.

Carson swiped his sunglasses off and dried them on the leg

of his flight suit. "I do have to get back to work, but I could pull together supper for you before I go. I haven't eaten today either, and I'm actually a competent cook."

"I know."

He stopped midswipe on a lens. "You do?"

Oops. Might as well fess up. He probably knew anyway and pretending she hadn't once followed him around like a silly puppy would only hint she still had feelings. While she might still have feelings, they sure weren't the tender kind anymore. "I used to pay all sorts of attention to what you did back during my 'crush' days."

His smile pulled tight. With guilt? He hooked his glasses on the neck of his uniform again. "So let me cook for you then."

Invite him into her apartment? Not a chance. "Thanks, but the drugs and the whole…everything…are still making me nauseous."

"Then I can sit and pass you crackers."

Definitely guilt.

She so didn't want him taking care of her out of obligation. "Thank you, but you have work. I have papers to grade and laundry to do. You've done enough already."

Understatement of the year.

She could see he wanted to argue…but his cell phone rang again. His forehead creased with frustration, his hand gravitating toward his phone even as he obviously battled the urge to ignore it.

"You know you can't ignore the call. Take it. I'll be fine."

And she would.

If only his intense blue eyes didn't shout that he wasn't done with her yet.

Chapter 3

He was done.

Carson leaned against the quarter panel of his truck and stared past the pool up at Nikki's apartment. She was safely inside, thank God. He'd walked her to the door. She hadn't invited him in—no surprise—but he'd waited until she assured him the place was safe and empty.

Now he could return to the pile of messages waiting for him at the squadron since he'd accomplished all he could from a cell phone for one day.

So why was he hanging out in a half-empty apartment parking lot, rain drizzling until it dripped from his hair onto his forehead? If he loitered around, staring up at Nikki's image moving around inside for much longer, somebody would call the cops on his ass. If he didn't freeze to death first even though he had his leather jacket back. Damned if the thing didn't smell like her now, a light flowery perfume and something unmistakably *her*. And double damn, but why could he still recognize her scent even after seven months?

He should just lose himself in work, order a deep-dish pizza and dig in for another 2:00 a.m. punch-out. Given the time change over in the Middle East, pulling a few extra hours at night worked well for speaking with the deployed squadron commander about routine business. Sure he could ask the new boss for advice on the whole mess, but the guy was swamped with duties overseas. Their old commander, Quade, had left two months ago and moved his family to the Pentagon for his next assignment, so he wasn't on hand to ask for advice, either.

Mentors were in short supply to help him out with this one. He was on his own in a job he hadn't asked for, wasn't even sure he was ready for yet. But the position had come to him anyway and he refused to screw it up.

The phone rang in his hand—again. He tucked the headset piece in his ear. "Major Hunt."

"Captain Lebowski from scheduling." The Chicago area accent cut through the earpiece. "We've got a problem I know you're going to find hard to believe, but when Reach 2-1-3-1 landed in Hawaii, the plane broke."

A broken plane and a crew in search of a tan. Great. Just what he needed today. "Yeah, amazing how that always happens on flights to Hawaii and never in Thule, Greenland. Let me guess on the ETTC—" estimated time to completion for a return home "—is a week right?"

"Of course it's a week. Who can get a decent tan in under a week?"

"All right, what's broken? Where's the part gotta come from? Do we need to ship maintenance guys out?"

Carson listened while continuing to scour the parking lot for—what? Something. Anything he could find that might be off and account for the mess of the past twelve hours. Because if he could find the cause, he could fix it like that broken plane.

He should drop his sorry butt into his truck and leave. He'd done more for her today than required, and the attention would not go unnoticed in his small community of aviators once word leaked of the incident.

So go.

And he would.

But he wouldn't stay gone, just checking from a distance. He owed Nikki for how he'd treated her. She'd been there for him at one of the lowest points of his life and he had taken without giving a thing back.

He understood all about the importance of making amends except when those amends might harm someone. He'd stayed away for seven months because being close to her again would only risk hurting her more.

Well, now staying away wasn't an option.

"And that's it, sir," Lebowski wrapped up his summary, "I'll give you a SITREP at the end of business."

A situation report to add to the list of work, but at least his people were on top of things.

"Roger and out."

He thumbed the off button, relieved it wasn't another major crisis. The ADO—assistant director of operations—directly below him in the chain of command could have handled this one, but the old commander Quade had been such a micromanager that the personnel around him hadn't broken the habit of calling about every nitnoid detail, which made the job more time-consuming than need be.

Quade was a helluva flyer, had been a dedicated commander, and no doubt cared about his people, even if his gruff demeanor implied otherwise on more than one occasion. But Carson had often wondered what would have happened to the squadron if Quade died while in charge.

Delegation was important. Sure there were times he could do the job better than someone less experienced, but if someone else could do the job well enough, that was okay, too. Otherwise how did anyone learn if they never had a chance to stretch their wings?

But what did he know? He was too damn young to be in this job anyway. Even with delegating, he was working his ass off so much he was lucky to get breakfast.

Or lunch.

He tucked the phone back in his thigh pocket and stared up at the balcony marking Nikki's place, her UNC alma mater flag waving beside her sliding doors. His chest went tight again as he thought about finding her this morning, her spine so straight while she sat wrapped in that blanket. He would do anything to wipe away this horror for her. Any-damn-thing. Nothing would slip his attention in this investigation. And hell, suddenly he understood Quade's position a little better.

Because Nikki's safety was one responsibility he couldn't bring himself to delegate.

Nikki brushed her hand over the stack of sixth grade reports on farming techniques of ancient Egypt calling to her for grades, but she resisted. Her students deserved her complete attention and a fully functioning brain.

She needed air, space, sun, all in short supply on this rainy day. But at least her balcony would be less claustrophobic than the tiny apartment that had seemed so big when she first moved in last fall.

Nikki snagged her cordless phone from the cradle and slid open the balcony door. She really craved a long run on the beach but her aching body probably wouldn't hold up for any length of time. Too bad the pool was closed for the winter. The water, chilly though it might be, invited from below.

Dropping into a lounger, she started to dial her mother's number when the phone rang in her hand before she could punch the first number.

She checked caller ID and found "Caller Unknown."

Her stomach clenched. Residual nerves, no doubt. She tapped the On button. "Yes?"

Silence stretched for a second too long. Her nerves flamed. She started to hang up and sprint back inside when a cleared throat on the other end stopped her.

"Nikki?"

Carson.

But he'd only just left. Standing, she scanned outside, past the swimming pool and found him three stories down in the parking lot, against the closed tailgate on his truck. She rested her elbows along the wooden rail, phone pressed to her ear as firmly as her eyes stayed locked on his tall, lean body.

"Did you forget something?" She'd returned his jacket, although she did still have his handkerchief.

"I seem to have overlooked doing one mighty damn important thing for too long."

The weight of his words seeped through the telephone. Did he intend for there to be a deeper meaning? Could he be referencing their night together after all these months? That evening she'd thought finally he'd noticed her only to have him leave the next morning and pretend the whole night never happened.

She wished she could erase that night from her memory as easily as she'd forgotten the one prior. "At least one of us has good recall today."

"I'm not talking about today."

"I know." How silly to speak on the phone while they looked at each other, but with a swimming pool between them and three stories of height, they were safe from touching.

Could he be as affected by her as she was by him? The disturbing and tempting thought spread soothing warmth through her on an oh-so-cold day. "Maybe we shouldn't talk right now with everything so jumbled—"

"I'm sorry for the way I behaved that night and the next morning."

An apology months too late.

She wouldn't be drawn in again. She couldn't bring herself to believe he was total scum, but something was messed up in that head of his and she didn't want any part of the fallout again.

Best to shoo him away fast before she did something reckless like ask him to come back up and inside. "You're forgiven."

"I don't deserve your forgiveness, but thank you."

She didn't want his gratitude. She wasn't sure what she

wanted—okay, she knew she'd always wanted Carson—but more than that she wanted to safeguard her heart so she wouldn't spend the next two decades mooning over a man as her mama had done.

"Thank you for your help today. I really need to go now. Goodbye."

She hung up fast, a clean break, as she should have done the first time Carson had smiled a hello at a squadron picnic years ago. Better yet, she turned away, back into her apartment. She wasn't a twenty-year-old hero worshipping the new guy on her father's crew anymore.

God, had she really had a thing for Carson for nearly three years?

Nikki angled through the half-open sliding door and dragged it closed, phone still clutched in her hand. Time to finally place that call to her mother. She punched in her parents' number and waited through *ring, ring, ring.*

"Hello?"

Chris. Her brother.

Her hands shook with adrenaline letdown along with the need to talk to somebody, and her brother was *so* the only person she could hang with right now. They'd forged a tight bond during all their family moves and their parents' marital troubles. She didn't care why Chris was back early from his New Year's road trip with college friends, but thank God he was.

She shouldn't drive anywhere because of the drug and nerves. Her brother could come over and pick her up. She couldn't stall telling her family any longer.

"Hey, runt. It's me. Could you come over? I've had a really crummy day."

* * *

His crappy day—hell, week—was finally about to end.

Carson gripped the stick on the C-17 and hurtled the craft through the sky closer to his home base. Only a couple more hours left until landing with the squadron representatives who'd flown out to Omaha for Owens's funeral.

He'd paid his respects to the family and worked like crazy not to think about the unanswered questions from the night the man had died. Still he couldn't help but wonder if Owens had been the one to drug Nikki's drink. And how had it happened at Beachcombers, the last place he would expect something like that to occur? Beachcombers wasn't some rave club, just a low-key seaside restaurant and bar where flyers hung out.

At least her brother was watching her and didn't seem to mind the occasional check-in call from Carson—under the guise of keeping tabs on J. T. Price's family while the man was deployed. He would continue checking in with Chris and with Special Agent Reis, while keeping his distance.

Game plan set, boots rocking the rudders, Carson lost himself in the sky as he soared the cargo plane through the clouds the way he escaped through hours spent skimming his thirty-one-foot Catalina sailboat over the waves.

Blue, blue and more blue…

He lived to fly, whether it was through the sky or along the ocean. That's all he'd ever wanted. He hadn't planned on a commander gig, but here he was, responsible for people like the crew around him.

Back in the cargo hold were loadmaster Picasso and in-flight mechanic Mako.

Up front in the cockpit, new baby copilot Kevin Avery sat in the right seat and instructor pilot Nola Seabrook was strapped in a jump seat behind them.

God, when had he gotten to be the old guy? Except he wasn't that much older than these aviators. Somehow he'd landed on the fast track—he hoped because of his ability. Although he often wondered if his prestige-hungry parents had played some of their behind-the-scenes games in their high-power circles with congressmen who happened to be close buddies with a general here or there.

The military wasn't supposed to operate that way, but the whole thing had spiraled beyond his control. So he worked his ass off to be the best damn pilot, officer, leader possible in order to be worthy of his commission and whatever responsibilities came his way. Including checking on Nikki.

And did everything have to cycle back around to Nikki Price?

Jesus, he needed to start seeing other women. Except he didn't have the time or interest in anyone else. Work overload and stress maxed him out. He knew his limits and he recognized the danger signs if he pushed himself to the wall. He was trying to lose himself in the sky, and would have to find time to sail soon. All to fight the urge to take what he really wanted and could never have again.

A drink.

Too many people counted on him. He couldn't risk screwing up. Stats read that every alcoholic's drinking affected at least four other lives. Any mistake he made would ripple through the whole squadron.

In spite of Nikki accepting his apology, what he'd done was unforgivable. He'd been so damn arrogant that night, thinking he was holding it together. That he was somehow stronger than his parents because he'd battled and won against *his* addiction.

His fall had been swift.

Attending his friend's wedding should have been low stress. Sure, drinks would flow, but he resisted that temptation every time he partied with his crewdog pals. He'd even hung out with his wartime crew before Spike's wedding. Life had finally been good again, the hell of their shoot down and capture in the Middle East past. He'd been cleared in the initial mandatory pysch eval. He knew with his family history he needed to be careful.

Then when he'd least expected it, everything flew apart. Why had seeing Spike that happy left him so damn shaken, enough to weaken and do something he'd been fighting for over a year not to do—hit on Nikki?

Next thing he'd known, he was looking at the bottom of an empty shot glass, then another, more following until…he couldn't remember more than spotty flashes of tangling naked with her in the sheets. Amazing flashes.

Flashes he also feared may have been brief and not nearly as good for her. Wasn't that a kick in the ego? And also a well-deserved punch to his good sense.

His fist clenched around the throttle. He fought the destructive urge to be with her every day. He couldn't offer her a damn thing, had tried to settle for friendship but knew now he couldn't go for half measures in any part of his life. He wasn't as strong at resisting temptation as he'd thought.

He had enough on his plate staying sober and doing his job. Speaking of which, he had a young pilot here in need of leading right now. Being an Air Force officer was about more than flying. He had a duty to train, mentor, motivate future leaders.

The failure with Owens weighed heavily on his shoulders today. He'd been certain the man was shaking his gambling problem. He'd even begun attending support meetings with other addicts.

Carson thumbed the interphone button. "Lieutenant Avery, let's talk. Career planning can never start too early. What's your goal?"

The wiry young pilot who probably weighed all of a hundred and thirty pounds soaking wet answered, "To be the Chief of Staff, sir."

Seabrook snorted into the headset from the jump seat. "Lieutenant, it may have escaped your notice, but since Curtis LeMay died, all the Chiefs of Staff have been fighter pilots."

"Oh." The scrawny kid deflated in his leather seat.

Damn. You'd think she stole the kid's ice-cream cone. "She has a point, but things change. Military transport is the fastest growing airframe, and we're raking in those medals. So you never know. What's your plan for making Chief of Staff?"

"I plan to be the best aviator I can be, sir."

Ambitions were all well and good, but he definitely needed to have a sit-down with this kid later about specific choices for different career paths, or before he knew it, he would be in a job he hadn't foreseen, either. "How about we settle on a more immediate goal today, with tangible early results."

"And what would that be, sir?"

"You tell me?" Take some initiative, kid. Having a goal

was great, but setting attainable immediate goals to get there was even more important. In the last three months, Carson had tried to be the mentor to Owens he hadn't found around himself near enough. A.A. meetings had taught him well the necessity of guidance and support, one-day-at-a-time steps.

"I'd like to earn a call sign, a cool one like yours, sir."

Avery thought the call sign "Scorch" was cool? Jesus, it came from the mortifying moment of setting his own mustache on fire with the flaming Dr Pepper drink in a bar.

Seabrook laughed, husky and slightly wicked. "So you're not enjoying the call sign always reserved for the newest aviator."

Avery winced. "No, ma'am."

"Then get to work earning a new name, Bambi."

Carson smothered a laugh at the lieutenant's shudder of disgust over the undignified moniker. "I'll keep my eye on you and see what new handle I can come up with."

"Thank you, sir. If it's okay, I'd like to step in back for a walk-around before landing."

"Roger, cleared to unstrap."

Bambi unbuckled the harness holding him in the copilot's seat and ducked out of the cockpit for the stairwell leading to the cargo hold. Captain Seabrook slid into the empty copilot's seat on the right and settled behind the stick, scanning the control panel. "Tough to believe we were once that idealistic."

"Maybe because we weren't." In those days his only plans centered around escaping his family legacy. The rigid structure of the military provided a blessed relief to a childhood spent not knowing what to expect from minute to minute with coke addict parents.

Lately he worried about the stress load sending him over the edge, something he was always on guard against and a part of why he kept his personal life as uncomplicated as possible. He dated, but low-key. He'd even dated Nola Seabrook three years ago, back when they were both Captains, when he was senior only in years and not her supervisor in any way. She was far more suited for him than Nikki, closer in age, they both understood the pressures of military life, combat, even captivity since Nola had been snatched during a mission in South America.

Jesus.

Surely the crappy-luck odds were about played out for them?

Of course now with his new promotion in the squadron, a relationship was out of the question even if he was interested. Which he wasn't, because the chemistry wasn't there in spite of her bombshell-blonde looks…and he couldn't shake a certain leggy brunette from his brain.

He definitely needed to keep his personal life simple for at least as long as the squadron stayed under his command. Lives depended on it.

Thank God the runway neared. Time to pull his attention back on landing this lumbering beast of a plane. An instant before he could thumb the radio button to contact the control tower, the headset squawked in his ears.

"Major Hunt, there's a message for you at the command post from Special Agent Reis. Something about an accident over at Nikki Price's place, a loose balcony railing."

His muscles clenched as tight as the knot of dread in his

gut. Screw having someone else check on her and keeping his distance. The second this plane touched down, he'd be out the hatch and on his way to Nikki's side. Where he intended to stay.

Chapter 4

Enough already.

Nikki considered herself a tough person overall, but had somebody painted a bull's-eye on her back while she wasn't looking?

She toed off the water faucet in her steaming bathtub that hadn't come close to easing the kinks and cold from her tumble off her balcony into the pool. At least she'd been able to control her fall enough to land in the water when the wooden railing gave way. Thank God for all those gymnastics classes her parents had paid for when she was a kid.

Her stomach still lurched just thinking about those horrifying seconds in midair. She rested her head back and wished she'd thought to turn on her stereo before she sank into the bubble bath. She could use all the help relaxing that she could scavenge.

Three stories was a helluva long way to fall and hope that the dive angle you'd taken would land you in the pool rather than smack you onto the cement instead. She'd no doubt made a record breaking cannonball splash. EMS techs called by her neighbor declared her unharmed, although she would be black-and-blue by morning.

What happened to her nice boring life? She was a junior high teacher whose biggest concern should have been whether or not her students made it to regionals for the history fair.

Her doorbell echoed.

Peace over.

She hauled herself out of the water and grabbed for her jogging shorts and T-shirt resting on the edge of the vanity.

The doorbell pealed again. Her mother, no doubt, since the gossipy little old man next door had called her family's house two seconds after phoning EMS. She really could have used a beach towel from him instead. It was darn cold in that pool in January, even in South Carolina.

When she'd told her mother about Gary's death, her mom had—no surprise—freaked. Nikki had calmed her down by tapping into her mother's training for suggestions on regaining her memory. Keeping a dream journal and making an appointment with a hypnotherapist didn't feel like much, but at least she was taking action, already unearthing snippets of memories.

When she wasn't busy diving off a third-floor balcony.

The doorbell stuttered while she tugged her clothes onto her damp body. "Hold on, hold on, Mom." She hopped, one leg at a time into shorts. "I'm coming and I'm gonna chew you out for not putting up your feet like the doctor—"

a building sneeze tingled through her sinuses, down her nose "—aaaachoo!"

She snitched Carson's freshly washed and folded handkerchief from the stack of laundry on her sofa and tried to ignore the teacher voice inside of her that insisted tissues were more sanitary than a cloth holding germs. And was this stuffy nose cosmic justice for lying to her mom about having a cold last week?

She tugged the door open. Rather than "concerned Mama," she found "pissed-off hunky flyboy." Her fingers fisted around the handkerchief, tucking her thumb to hide the telltale corner peeking out.

Carson gripped the door frame, his sensuous lower lip pulling tight. "You're okay."

"You don't have to sound so mad about it."

His hand slid from the frame and before she could blink— or head back into her apartment away from temptation—he hauled her to his chest. "Jesus, Nikki, you could have died. I damn near had a heart attack when command post patched through an in-flight call about this."

Hunky, awesome-smelling flyboy, who'd raced straight over after a flight just for her. Muscle, leather and all that concern made for a heady sensory combination, especially when she was already susceptible to this man. Her body obviously wasn't near as smart as her mind.

But her will was stronger. She edged her shoulders free, stepping back without meeting his eyes. "I landed in the pool." What was she doing staring at her bare feet beside his boots? She forced her gaze up to meet his full on, no flinching.

His hand gravitated to her damp hair. "How long ago did it happen if your hair's wet?"

She held still under his touch, the heat of his fingers steaming her skin from a simple brush of his knuckles across her cheek. Better to let him think the water was from her impromptu swim than mention she was naked in the tub sixty seconds ago. "Why did they call you?"

His hand fell away. "Your mother phoned my secretary at the squadron to track me down. She wanted me to check on you since her doctor has her on bed rest."

"Figures." Where was Chris when she needed him? "You'd think I was still in college."

"I think you're lucky to have a family who cares. Was she a little intrusive? Maybe. But I don't see her here hovering."

"You're right. I am lucky, and I don't mean to sound like a brat."

She might not want a relationship with him anymore, but her ego still nudged her to be careful. They were inching toward dangerous—tempting—territory every time they spoke.

He strode past. She grabbed the door frame to support her suddenly shaky knees.

She watched him saunter into her apartment, a place he'd never stepped inside before. Seven months ago she'd been finishing up at UNC. Their one night together had been at his place, a beach community bungalow he'd bought from another military family when they'd moved.

She wondered what he thought of her bargain-basement Pier 1 knockoffs and the scattered plants she'd grafted from her mother's garden in an attempt to fill corners she couldn't afford to decorate.

Why was she thinking about appearances now when she'd never cared about material things before? If Carson Hunt— obviously from wealth—was only impressed by a price tag, then she was well rid of him.

He stopped short in front of her class's latest history project. "What the hell is this?"

She laughed and damn it felt good, almost as good as the rush because he'd noticed her most prized possession in the whole place. Her students had crafted the towering project which made it worth gold to her. Nikki walked deeper into the apartment, surreptitiously hiding the used handkerchief under a throw pillow until she could wash it.

Nikki tugged a tissue from the end table on her way to the six-foot-high papier-mâché creation she'd brought home from school strapped into the back of her Ford Ranger. "It's a sarcophagus."

"Ohhh-kay." Hands hooked in the pockets of his leather flight jacket, he studied the psychedelic coffin propped against the island counter separating the small kitchen from the rest of the dining area. "While I don't claim to be an interior design expert, why do you have one in your dining room?"

She ambled closer, determined not to bemoan the fact she was wearing nothing but ratty gym shorts and a threadbare T-shirt over her damp body. "My students are studying Egyptian history. The kids have been crafting papier-mâché items to go in the tomb, and we tried to build this in class, too, but Trey Baker spilled his lunch inside the sarcophagus and tapioca pudding totally stinks when it rots, so I had to cut that part out. Although what kid actually eats tapioca? Most children I know like chocolate pudding with candy sprinkles or gummies, or maybe a cookie crumbled on top."

"I liked tapioca when I was a kid."

"Geez, were your parents health food nuts or what?"

"Or what."

Welcoming the chuckle, she leaned an elbow against the counter bar and smoothed down a straggly corner of newspaper sticking from the still-damp section. "Anyhow, I'm patching over where I cut out the damaged part."

She'd taken a break from repairing the project to eat supper out on her balcony. Memories of Carson's apology had drawn her to the railing and before she'd known it, she was tumbling heart over butt toward the pool. "It should be dry enough to paint by tomorrow."

"Shouldn't you be resting?"

Reasonable notion except every time she closed her eyes she saw Gary Owens's vacant dead stare. "If I rest, I'll think. I'd rather work. Although building a coffin really isn't helping take my mind off this whole mess."

"Rather macabre."

"Macabre." She snatched up a piece of paper from under the phone.

"What are you doing?"

"Writing down the word." And trying to think about anything but the dead man and unanswered questions. She finished scrawling on the notepaper and tore the top sheet off from the soccer-patterned pad—a Christmas gift from one of her pupils. "I've got this student who's a word wizard. Feeding his brain is a full-time job. You use these words that are not the kind guys would usually choose."

"I can't decide if you're insulting or complimenting me."

"Neither. You just don't speak as informally as most guys I know."

"I'm older than most guys you know. Hell, I even eat tapioca, remember? If I said dude a couple of times, you wouldn't notice the other words."

"Still hung up on being a cradle robber, are you?"

His eyebrows shot up at her open acknowledgement of their past relationship. Relationship? One-night stand.

Ouch.

He thumbed the pad of paper, fanning through sheets until one piece peeled loose. "Shouldn't you be resting?"

"You already said that."

"Must be early onset Alzheimer's at thirty-five." Absently he picked up the stray piece of paper, leaned back against the bar and started folding. "I understand you need to keep your mind off things, but how about reading a book? Your body has been through hell the past few days. You should take care of yourself."

"I'm a young, resilient twenty-three, not an *old* thirty-five like you."

He stopped midfold on the soccer paper. "I'm guessing your mother and father encouraged you to speak your mind when you were a kid."

"What clued you in?" She smirked for a full five-second gloat before the fun faded with reality. "And how surprising that you always manage to bring up my dad anytime we speak."

"People have parents."

"You don't."

"Sure I do." His fingers started tucking and folding the paper again, drawing her eyes to his talented nimble hands.

Hands she remembered feeling over her skin too well right now. "Other than our tapioca conversation, you've never mentioned your parents once in all the time I've known you."

"I didn't crawl from under a rock."

She smiled slow and just a little bit impishly vindictive. "That's open for debate."

His laugh rumbled low and long, wrapping around her with far more languorous warmth than the ineffective bubble bath she'd stepped out of ten short minutes ago. Her body tingled with awareness, her breasts suddenly oversensitive to the brush of cotton against her bare skin.

"Damn, Nikki, you never did cut me any slack." Shaking his head with a final self-derisive laugh, he bent a last tuck on the paper and extended his hand to her with the finished product cradled in his palm—an origami bird.

She inched backward, then caught herself. This was her home, her life. She stood taller and stood him down. "Stop trying to be charming."

His beautiful smile and laugh faded to a mere echo. "I thought you accepted my apology."

"I did." She wadded the tissue in her hand, tossing it aside with a final sniffle. Cold. Not tears. No more tears over this man. "But you can drop the charming friend act. There's no going back to how things were. You had your chance, and you blew it, dude."

His mouth went tight, his eyes dropping away from hers. Pausing. Holding. Right at her shirt level.

A damp T-shirt she now realized clung to her breasts that happened to be hyperaware of the sexy blond hunk standing a reach away.

Carson's hands shook from resisting the urge to reach for Nikki and cup her breasts that he happened to know fit perfectly in his palms.

And damn it all, why did he have to remember the feel and taste and texture of her in his mouth right now? Washed-thin cotton clung to her skin and subtle curves, begging to be peeled up and off so he could dip his head and lick away whatever water remained on her skin.

Water.

He needed to remember what had happened tonight, how she'd almost plunged to her death, would have if not for the pool below. The thought alone served as an effective cold splash on his heated body. That railing shouldn't have given way. This was a new complex with pristine upkeep. He couldn't ignore the possibility that someone could have tampered with the balcony rail, someone who didn't want her to remember what happened that night in Owens's VOQ room.

He could be wrong, but it was a helluva lot safer to err on the side of caution. "You shouldn't stay here by yourself."

Her spine went straighter, which just so happened to press her peaked breasts tighter against the T-shirt. Counting to ten—twenty—he set the origami bird on the counter.

She folded her arms across her chest. "If you're offering to hang out with me, I'll have to decline."

"I never thought you would agree to that anyway. And quite frankly, I don't think it would be wise."

She bristled to her full five feet ten inches tall. "Because you're afraid I'll jump your bones? Well, you can be sure that even if I'd been the least bit tempted before, you've killed that spark."

Heard. Understood. And regretted.

"I'm more concerned with my own self-control." The words tumbled out ahead of his better sense. Not really a surprise considering how he always seemed to lose his head around this leggy dynamo who could outrace most men and kept a sarcophagus in her living room.

Her jaw dropped wide, started to close then went slack again. A bracing sigh later, she answered, "I don't know what you're expecting to accomplish with a comment like that, but you made it clear the morning after Spike's wedding that you don't want me in your life, and you didn't do it in a particularly nice way. If you had a sister—"

"I do."

"You do?"

Her jaw went slack again, tempting him to kiss the surprise right off her face. Coming here had really been a mammothly stupid idea.

But before he could drag his sorry, horny butt out the door she continued, "Quit distracting me. My point is, if someone treated your sister the way you treated me, you would kick his ass."

"You're right." More than she could even know. He shoved away from the counter and her too-cute sarcophagus and idealistic too-young heart. "And since I don't want *my* ass kicked by your brother or father, it's best I don't stay here. I just had to see for myself that you're okay and make sure you're safe."

Did she have to look so damn conflicted? He was having a tough enough time resisting her when she told him to shut up with all that fire and spunk he knew she brought to bed with her.

She skirted around the sofa full of inviting green pillows that would spread perfectly along the carpet to make a downy lawn for all-night sex. "Good night then. Have a nice drive home."

"Fine, but you're not staying here, either."

Nikki stopped short. "Why do I feel the irrepressible urge to put my hands over my ears and shout, 'You're not the boss of me'? Of course that would fit right in with your whole too-young-for-you mantra."

God, he liked her sense of humor. "You're good."

She snorted. "That compliment came about seven months too late."

"I meant at distracting *me*."

"Apparently not nearly good enough." She sagged to sit on the arm of the sofa. "Why are you so gung-ho on my not being alone?"

"With everything that happened with Owens, I'm concerned your balcony railing giving way might not have been an accident." He planted his boots deep in the plush carpet, the need to see her safe burning even stronger than the need to see her naked.

God, she hated being afraid of her own shadow.

But Carson's words kept rolling around in her head the next day as she parked her small truck in her parents' driveway. Late-afternoon sun dappled through the evergreens packing the yard surrounding the two-story white wood home.

She'd brushed aside Carson's concerns the night before, told him she would double bolt her door and think about what he'd said. She'd bristled out of pride and a need for independence.

Stupid. Stupid. Stupid.

About halfway through her PowerBar at lunch, she'd come to the conclusion that safety was too important. She wouldn't be one of those airheads in a horror movie who went walking in the dark woods at night even when half her friends had already been whacked by some psycho with a gas-powered garden tool.

So here she was with her truck and a suitcase full of clothes. She didn't need a reality check. She already knew. Bad crap was happening. Gary was very dead and she'd darn near died falling off her balcony. Even if it was an accident, she would have been more alert to her surroundings before this mess. Until she could get her life settled again, she needed to be extra careful.

Her mother was worried anyway and in need of extra help with her difficult pregnancy. Why not take her up on the standing offer to stay in the garage apartment?

She could still come and go as she pleased, but would have her brother nearby. Sure sometimes he'd been a wormy little pest who once dumped all her makeup into the sewer. But now that he'd shot up to six foot four inches, he made a fairly decent crime deterrent.

And she sure had plenty of time on her hands to help her mom repaint the new nursery.

Her principal had suggested she take a weeklong vacation. *Suggested* being a loose way of putting it. She suspected a parent or two had complained after getting wind of what happened the night Gary died. Whatever *had* happened.

Gossip could be hell. As much as she wanted to dig her heels in, she could see the principal's resolve. Pissing off her boss now wouldn't be wise.

Her whole life was crashing down around her. She needed control over something. At least she could still tutor her at-risk high schoolers or she would go nuts.

She threw open her truck door, stepped out and reached into the back to heft up her suitcase. Carson was right. She was lucky to have a family support system. Her parents had worked hard to build this for their kids and finally for themselves, too. She wouldn't settle for anything less when it came to building her own life.

And suddenly she couldn't help but wonder what sort of childhood had Carson had. He'd mentioned a sister and a love of tapioca, but nothing else.

Before she could tap on the screen, the front door swung open. Her tiny mother stepped into view with an unmistakable belly and a headful of dark curls lightly streaked with silver. "Nikki!" She swung the door wider, her gaze skating to the suitcase on the plank porch. "I'm so glad you decided to take me up on the offer of some pampering."

"The garage apartment—no pampering, though, please. I was hoping I could help paint the nursery." She reached to pat her mother's stomach and stifled thoughts of having kids of her own. Now definitely wasn't the time. "How's my little sister?"

"She's doing—" Her mother paused, eyes narrowing. "Wait. How did you know it's a girl? Did your father spill the beans in spite of our decision to wait to tell everyone when he gets home?"

Nikki pulled her hand back and hefted her suitcase. "Lucky guess. I figured I had a fifty-fifty shot of getting it right and tripping you up."

"Brat." She swatted her arm with her gardening magazine. "Your father always did spoil you."

"And you need some spoiling today, too. Now how about put your feet up and I'll come down to check on you once I stow my gear over the garage?"

Nikki backed down the steps and over to the outside stairs leading to the garage apartment her father had modified. If her dad was here now, no doubt J. T. Price would worry about everything with Owens. He was concerned enough with what few details he'd been told.

Her father was overprotective, always had been. She'd actually felt sorry for the poor skinny high school boys who made it to her front porch only to be confronted by her six-foot-four-inch weight lifter father. He didn't scowl. But he didn't smile at those fellas, either.

What a sucky welcome home he would have if she didn't get this mess straightened out. While she wasn't some woman in desperate need of daddy's approval, she also wasn't overly thrilled at the prospect of worrying or disappointing him, either.

One day at a time. She would have to trust the OSI and Special Agent Reis to do their job.

Meanwhile, the best thing she could do for her parents—and for herself—was keep life level, help her mother out with some yard work. Not stress about what she couldn't control.

Her cell phone buzzed in her black backpack purse slung over her shoulder, and with an instinctive awareness she didn't want and couldn't escape, she knew it was Carson checking up on her again.

Chapter 5

"Hello, Major, what can I help you with?"

Carson stepped deeper into the OSI agent's office, hoping for a few answers from Reis, who was currently slipping a tie over his head and tightening it to start his day. The guy stored ties in his office? A kindred workaholic, which boded well for solving this case faster.

And please God, clearing Nikki.

She hadn't answered his phone calls in two days, but he couldn't blame her. She'd left a message for him with his secretary, insisting she didn't need to speak to him directly, but that she was fine and staying at her mom's.

At least she was camping out where her college-aged brother could keep his eyes open. Carson refused to feel guilty for checking in with Chris, any more than he would feel guilty about stopping in to fact-check with Reis. "I'm here for an update on the Owens case and anything you may have uncovered about Nikki Price's accident."

His gut still burned from even thinking about Nikki plummeting from that balcony.

Distraction. He needed it. Pronto. So he studied the room for hints about this man who held Nikki's life in his investigative hands.

Framed soccer field posters from around the world splashed the walls with color—one even including a photo of Reis with a soccer trophy and bottle of champagne. He didn't need to avert his eyes from the liquor as he had in the early days on the wagon.

He could even remember now how Cabernet had been his vino of choice with steaks and Pinot Noir had accompanied him on more than a few sailing trips. He didn't crave as he used to, but the thoughts still crowded his mind.

Reis shoved aside an old carryout box marked from a gourmet deli. "How's Ms. Price doing after her tumble from the balcony?"

"Fine, barely rattled other than a cold from the freezing water."

"So you've spoken to her?"

Why was he asking? Reis probably already knew anyway. Carson avoided the question and simply stated, "Seems mighty coincidental to me, her railing giving way."

"Could be an accident."

"Or it could be someone trying to kill her before she remembers what happened."

"Do ya' think?" Reis quirked an eyebrow.

What an ass. But being openly antagonistic in return

wouldn't get the answers he needed. "Excuse me for being slow on the uptake, but I fail to see what's so damn funny."

Reis rocked back in his chair underneath an autographed photo of Pelé. "What's so damn funny? Watching you, Major. I've seen you work a crisis without flinching, with a calm I'd expect from someone more seasoned. But when it comes to a woman, you're just as human as the rest of us."

Well hell. While it might be true—all right, *was* true— what did this have to do with anything? He'd be irritated if he didn't admire the guy's no-bull attitude and sharp eye. "Call me Cro-Magnon, but it pisses me off when a woman— any woman—is in danger. It's my job to protect. I can't turn that off just because I'm not in combat."

"That's the only reason I'm not chewing your ass for thinking I'm idiot enough not to have considered the possibility someone may have tampered with her balcony. There're plenty of reasons somebody may have been angry enough to whack Owens over the head. His gambling habit. Or maybe Nikki Price had a jealous ex-boyfriend who didn't much like her getting busy with another guy."

An understandable possibility since thinking about Nikki dating other guys tossed acid onto his already burning raw gut even though he had no claim to her. He kept his hands loose, his face impassive. He'd mastered the blasé look with his new command duties.

Funny thing, though, Reis was giving him exactly the same blank expression. The investigator's words about ex-boyfriends being to blame shifted in Carson's head, settling into place a second before Reis leaned forward, elbows on his desk.

"So I guess you won't be surprised to hear you're on my suspect list, as well, Major."

How damned ironic that in spite of years of working to hide his attraction to Nikki, the agent had pegged it so fast.

If he was doing such a piss-poor job of keeping his emotions under wraps, then maybe it was time to confront this dogged attraction head-on with Nikki after all.

Nikki jogged alongside her brother, her running shoes pounding pavement with dogged determination. She shot puffy clouds of air ahead then plowed through the vapor. Too bad her cloudy memories weren't as easily dispersed.

Thank goodness Chris didn't want to talk because she had too much energy to work out. Instead, she kept her Walkman headset in place, hoping exhaustion and WWII era tunes—The Andrews sisters at present—would soothe her frustration over having her life hijacked.

She missed her apartment and independence. However as much as she wanted to return to her place and simply invest in a kick-ass security system, she couldn't forget her mother's strained face and difficult pregnancy. Her father was due home in another week. She could put her own needs on hold for a few more days.

Cars chugged past in the sleepy neighborhood, some turning around and taking detours for ongoing road construction, but she felt safe enough in the late afternoon with her brother alongside. Even Carson couldn't expect her to hole up inside indefinitely.

One foot in front of the other, she willed the runner's high to overtake her so she could block out the resurrected yearning to be with Carson, a light harmonic melody pulsing through her ears and thrumming in her veins. A swelling, sentimental ache she'd finally acknowledged the night she decided to break things off with Gary...

Nikki thudded along the planked boardwalk stretching toward Beachcombers Bar and Grill. Flight-jacket-clad bodies with dates packed the back porch, twice as many undoubtedly inside if the dull roar was anything to gauge by. Finding Gary could take hours in this wash of brown leather and jeans. Better to park her butt at the bar and wait for him to find her.

A marshy breeze blew in off the beach, cold, but not enough to drive the congregated smokers back inside. She charged closer while sailboats bobbed along the nearby marina, lines snapping and pinging against masts in a mariner's tune.

But she wouldn't be lured by that song of Carson anymore. Tonight would be her fresh start. No more self-destructive dating losers who happened to resemble Carson.

One of the first things on her agenda, stop coming to a watering hole populated with flyboys from nearby Charleston Air Force Base. Climbing the steps up to the hangout housed in a historic clapboard two story, she pushed the rest of the way through, smiling and nodding at familiar faces she barely registered. Same old crowd, even on a Sunday evening.

The bass from the band pulsed through the ground, beach music blending with old rock tunes from her parents' day that had round-robined back into modern remakes. She sucked in a bracing breath, prepping herself for the upcoming confrontation. Gary had been a little possessive in the past when guys hit on her, but not violent. Still just in case, she'd chosen a public meeting place.

She parted a circle playing quarters. "Pardon me. 'Scuse me." She ducked around an overendowed regular wearing Lycra and no coat in January. "Excuse me, Hannah."

Finally. The door.

Nikki dodged another couple between her and her destination—and slammed into a solid body. Her senses announced his identity before she even looked up.

Carson, full of musky scent mixed with a fresh ocean air, unmistakably him. She forced her gaze upward and her feet to stomp backward when she wanted to stay smack-dab where she was and just breathe for a few minutes—or days.

"Hi, Scorch."

She refused to duck and run. She had nothing to be ashamed of. He was the one who'd been a total jerk and if speaking with her made him a smidge uncomfortable, then too damn bad.

He hitched a foot on the step back into the main bar, shoulder on the door frame, a white paper sack clutched in his hand. "Hey, have you spoken with your father recently?"

And wasn't that just like him to bring up her dad every time they spoke? Thinking Carson stayed away because of her father stung a little less, since at least he had a reason—albeit a really stupid one. However if he'd simply been a user-jerk, then getting over him would be easier.

A lose-lose situation for her.

"Phone calls have been scarce, but the Internet has been awesome. He talks more through e-mail than he would over the phone anyhow."

"That's your dad."

"Are you meeting someone here?" Ah hell.

"No, just grabbing carryout on my way to a meeting." He lifted his hand gripping the paper sack. "Nothing like Claire's Southern barbecue wings after a day of sailing."

Claire McDermott was joint owner of Beachcombers with her sisters. Claire was a single attractive woman who happened to cook Carson's favorite food—and didn't jealousy suck? The guy was heading to a late meeting at work on a Sunday night, for goodness' sake. "So you're still sailing."

"I finally bit the bullet and replaced my old sixteen-footer with a used thirty-one-foot Catalina a couple of months ago."

She could so see him out on the water, sun bleaching his golden hair white, bronzing his chest while they both savored the waves and the day. She'd always admired his way of enjoying silence as much as a conversation. "Good for you. Life should be lived."

He stared back at her with eyes so blue she saw the ocean and really wanted to jump in, headfirst, no safety preserver.

He blinked first—thank God—and looked over her shoulder. "Are you meeting someone?"

She wanted to say no and see if he asked her to join him for supper, but she was smart enough not to act on that "want" with this man ever again. "Yeah, he should be here any minute."

His sky-blue eyes blanked. "I won't keep you then."

"Enjoy your wings and your meeting."

Nodding, he brushed past and heaven help her she watched his confident long strides since he couldn't see her unrestrained attention as he melded into the crowd. And how weird was it that suddenly she could see through that crowd just fine when it came to watching him?

Pain—and yes, anger—whispered through her veins. All of which strengthened her resolve to break things off with Gary. How unfair to date him when she still had this mess of feelings for Carson tangled tighter than those sailboat lines twisting in the wind.

He cleared the walkway and stopped. Waving?

She should look away. Leave. Quit staring after him like a lovesick dork. And she would in just a second.

Carson called to someone behind a beat-up truck but his words drifted away on the wind and out to sea. He waited to be joined by two men—an older, shorter man in a backward ball cap and another guy about Carson's age, taller in a plaid shirt. She couldn't make them out well from a distance and didn't study them overlong since she was too busy being more relieved than she should that Carson wasn't with a woman.

He walked with the two men toward his extended-cab truck where they all three climbed in. All? Apparently there wasn't a work meeting after all. It stung more than a little that he'd felt the need to make excuses.

Definitely time to leave and move forward...

Panting from her run, Nikki slowed on the sidewalk in front of her parents' next-door neighbor's, sifting through the mishmash of emotions from that night to simply analyze the event.

She'd already remembered that time prior to stepping inside, but relaxing did offer her a few more details—like the two men Carson met up with. Problem was that seemed so insignificant. She could only hope the relaxation techniques suggested by the hypnotist would help her recall more.

As if she'd conjured Carson from her thoughts, there he was, in the driveway with her mother, little Jamie barreling by the trailer hitch on his toddler scooter.

Her mom sagged back against the fender of Carson's truck, her hand pressed to her forehead. Nikki's stomach lurched up to her throat. Had something happened to her father? God, she'd been so selfishly focused on her own mess she'd all but forgotten that her dad was in the Middle East, not a safe place for military members on the ground or in the air.

Nikki ripped the headset from her ears and sprinted across the dormant lawn, over a low hedge toward her mother. "Mom?" She took her mother's elbow, determined to keep it together, be supportive. "I'm here. Breathe—"

"It's all right," Rena interrupted, straightening with a shaky smile. "Everything's fine. I only got a smidge spooked when Scorch drove up. I had a little flashback to the other time my husband's commander showed up on my doorstep. Of course I know you wouldn't come alone for a bad call. You would bring along a doctor and chaplain," she rambled, gasping. "But still…"

Carson jammed his fists into his leather coat pockets. "I'm sorry. I didn't mean to scare you. I just came to check on everyone. And you're right. I wouldn't be here alone and I wouldn't be wearing a flight suit."

He would wear his dress blues, all those ribbons across his chest. He could be a poster model for a recruiting office he filled out any uniform so well. What a silly superficial thought that made her wonder if her feelings were still the result of physical attraction and the old crush.

She didn't much like what that said about her.

He'd apologized, hadn't made excuses and seemed to be working on amends. Just because she didn't totally trust him, she didn't have to be rude. And the excitement circling laps around inside her stomach was simply nerves because of their history. Maybe she'd gotten it wrong over the past seven months by staying away from him. Perhaps spending more time with him would help her get over that.

Get over *him*.

He had to stop looking at *her* before her family noticed.

But Carson couldn't seem to reel in his attention from Nikki, her face glistening with sweat, her hair mussed, much like he imagined she would look during marathon sex. Which he would give his left nut to remember having had with her seven months ago.

The next morning, they'd been naked in bed together and he couldn't even recall shedding more than their shirts. He remembered well that incredible moment she'd unfastened the front clasp of her bra, freeing perfect pert breasts. He'd reached for her with both hands, could feel the shape and pebbling peaks of her against his palms even now.

His breathing hitched right along with a skipped heartbeat. How idiotic to think about sleeping with Nikki when standing in the driveway with her exhausted mother, worried brother and wild man baby brother currently trying to run over Carson's boots with his scooter.

Actually, it wasn't wise to think about getting naked with her at any time, because his self control was dwindling fast the longer he spent with her. But he'd figured out quickly in Reis's office that he wasn't fooling anyone, especially himself, by staying away. Best to convince her they could resurrect the light friendship they'd once had.

While keeping his flight suit zipped this time.

Nikki's brother Chris shuffled up beside them, his eyes locked on his mother's weary face, concern stamping a maturity beyond his years on his college-aged features. The kid had been bending over backward to help out around the house since his own brush with the law his junior year in high school. His part-time job at a restaurant then had almost turned deadly when the boy's boss had tried to use Chris as cash mule for drug money.

Damn, hadn't the Price family been through enough?

"Hey, Mom?" Chris cupped her elbow. "How about we go inside and I'll dig up some of that chocolate peanut butter and marshmallow ice cream you've been craving?"

Rena straightened from the car, her gaze shifting from Carson to her daughter and back again with too much perception for his comfort level. Rena tucked her hand in the crook of her lanky son's elbow. "That sounds wonderful, Chris. Then Scorch can finish, uh, *checking* on Nikki."

Nikki shifted from foot to foot, fidgeting in a way he recognized as her need to run. He completely sympathized, which steeled his resolve to make this right between them.

Carson tapped the earphones dangling around her neck, soft strains of something filtering through but unidentifiable. "What's playing?"

A smile teased at her full lips, no gloss needed. She had a shine all her own. "Want to guess?"

"Lady, I couldn't figure you out if I had a million guesses."

"Thanks, I think." She reached down to the CD player

clipped to her Lycra running pants and turned off the music. "My secret shame—I'm a big band, WWII music addict. Ragtime, too. Anything over sixty years old, and I'm there."

"God, you're full of surprises." How odd to realize he didn't know her any better than she knew him. He thought he'd been the one with all the secrets.

"That's me, unpredictable as ever, although I have to confess that these days I'm in the mood for a boring life."

The past few days had to have been scary as hell for her. Carson cupped her elbow, which seemed surprisingly frail even through the thick cotton of her pullover and a body he knew to be toned from running, workouts and even her membership on a local rec league soccer team. Thank heaven for those honed quick reflexes. Still, she had to be sore, bruised maybe.

He searched for signs of scrapes but found nothing visible. "Are you okay? You look tired."

She scrunched her elegant nose. "Thanks."

"Are you feeling any aftereffects from the fall? You didn't actually go into work today, did you?"

"I wish. But no work for me today. The principal thinks it's best I take a couple of weeks off."

"What the f—" He stopped short, biting back the word along with his anger at the injustice before shoving it all aside to focus on her. "I'm so damn sorry."

"Me, too. The principal was hanging tough until word leaked that DNA tests of the skin under Gary's fingernails matched mine, which of course still doesn't mean a thing since I was obviously there with him."

His jaw flexed with tension or—more unsettling—jealousy? "Having your life on hold must be hell."

"They're paying me, so I shouldn't complain, but my students…" She shook her head, ponytail swishing from the back of her Atlanta Braves ball cap. "I wanted to be there with them when they present at the regional history fair."

"The sarcophagus."

"At least we got to finish the display and the reports before my surprise vacation." She nodded toward the open garage door full of gardening supplies. "I'm keeping busy around here in the meantime. I figure I can sabotage most of Mom's gorgeous landscaping by the end of the week."

The perfect excuse to hang around here longer and launch his plan to resurrect their unlikely friendship.

"Want some help? For your dad, of course." He winked.

Snorting, she rolled her eyes. "You're picking on me, aren't you?"

"More than a little."

"I think I lost my sense of humor along with a few hours of my life." She scooped a second sweatshirt off the hood of her truck and tugged it over her head on her way to the garage. She could pull on five layers and his mind's eye would see the beauty underneath, his hands itching to tunnel inside for a second sampling.

"About my dad—" she sidestepped a table saw on her way to the wheelbarrow "—I had to tell him what's going on before the news filtered over there."

He walked up alongside her in the garage, the scent of motor oil arousing as hell when mixed with a hint of Nikki's soap. "That must have been tough."

"Totally sucked." She passed him a rake. "I was so proud of myself for being independent, and yet, here I am."

She emptied the wheelbarrow, tossing two bags of mulch on the cement floor and grabbing the handles to roll it outside. Empty oak branches swayed overhead along with evergreens. She'd run a couple of miles and now planned to cool down with yard work? This woman really did need a friend's support more than maybe even she knew.

"Independence doesn't mean stupidity." He scraped the rake over the yard, gathering a growing tidal wave of dead pine needles. "It's good, normal and damned lucky to have family you can count on who know they can count on you."

"What about your family?" She knelt to scoop up the growing pile of pine straw with her hands. "You mentioned a sister."

"My sister's married, lives with her husband in Ireland."

"Ireland? Wow, you don't hear that one all that often."

He rubbed his thumb against two fingers in the universal "money" symbol.

"Ah, lucky for them."

He shrugged, raking faster. The Prices seemed a helluva lot richer to him with their overflowing home and working class values.

She stared up as she rose to take the handles again. "The whole 'money doesn't buy happiness' notion? Hmmm… maybe not, but it sure pays the bills." She dumped the full wheelbarrow by the curb and rolled back to his next pile of straw. "What about the rest of your family?"

"Well, they don't have any problems meeting their bills."

"You have that look to you."

"That look?" He peered over his aviator glasses, liking the *look* of her so much it was tough to process her words.

"Prep school education. A far cry from my parents' garage jam-packed full of yard gear, greasy tools and workout weights."

Her implied censure gave him pause. He'd always known she had a crush on him. He knew he had his faults—big ass faults—but since she didn't know about his alcoholism, he'd never stopped to consider there might be other things she disapproved of about his way of life. That tweaked more than it should have. "I think you're insulting me."

"No. Only commenting on our obvious differences. Just because I feel you did a really scumbag thing a few months ago doesn't mean I believe you're an actual scumbag."

"Thanks." Sort of.

"But while we're on the subject of that really scumbag thing you did for which you have finally apologized but never explained…" She dumped another load of pine straw, her face averted a little too conveniently to be coincidence.

"Noticed that, did you?" He leaned on the rake, taking in the overstiff brace of her shoulders and wanting to kick his own ass.

"Tough not to notice." She slumped back against the tree, hands behind her. "So why did you walk out the door and never bother to call? Or better yet, why did you invite me through your door in the first place?"

And into his bed. That much, at least, he remembered along with the feel of her bare chest against his as they'd tumbled onto the mattress. He'd just lost most of the parts between bed and waking up. The good parts, stolen by a drunken blackout. Finding Nikki naked next to him in the morning and knowing he'd broken her trust, her father's trust and his own code of honor made him realize he'd bottomed out.

He'd rolled his sorry, hungover butt off the mattress and found an Alcoholics Anonymous chapter. A.A. meetings had saved his life. Slowly, he was regaining his self-respect.

One day at a time. Never take it for granted.

"Why did I go to bed with you?" The truth wouldn't hurt any worse. He flattened a hand to the tree beside her head and let what he was thinking and feeling show for the first time in…he couldn't remember when. "Because I really wanted to be there, for a long time, almost from the first time I saw you. You were legal, but damn, you were young. And on that day, I was truly too much of a scumbag to stay away—"

"Stop." She clapped a hand to his mouth.

"Stop?" Speaking felt too much like kissing her hand, which messed with his head more than any drink.

"I've changed my mind." Her hand trembled. "I don't want to hear this tonight. I want to rake leaves and talk like we used to." Her hand fell away.

Her soft touch lingered, a simple caress when they'd shared far more overtly sexual touches and still he went stone hard, wanting her so much his teeth hurt. "Before you realized I'm a scumbag?"

"Yeah."

Wasn't that what he'd wanted as well in coming here tonight? So go. Leave. "Do you think you can really forget what I did that night?"

"I can forget for an evening."

Less than he'd hoped for but more than he deserved. "Fair enough."

Since she didn't move away he let himself keep staring into her eyes. What could happen outside in her parents' front yard while traffic inched past? Branches rustled overhead raining more pine straw around them, some catching in her hair. He lifted his hand and still she didn't move away, apparently as caught in this insanity as he was. He swept his fingers over her head. Silky strands. So damn soft that before he knew it he'd cupped the base of her skull.

Her pupils went wide, her gray eyes stormier still until he could have sworn the sun was sinking faster. So easily he could urge her closer. Or step forward. Or hell, just lean and taste her because it killed him, absolutely freaking killed him, that he only had spotty recollections of what happened between them that night.

He would give anything to have at least the memory of those lost hours. Although he suspected remembering would torment him even more.

The front door blasted open a second ahead of her brother Chris loping through onto the porch. "Mom sent me out to ask if Carson would like to stay for supper?"

A mom probably smart enough to realize things needed breaking up out front before he snapped the thin thread of Nikki's returning trust.

Carson backed away, shoving his hands in his pockets. He didn't deserve that trust, but he would be damned if he would abuse it again. As much as he wanted to climb those steps and hang out with this awesomely normal family and listen to Nikki's even more amazing laugh, he knew better now. He'd made a step in reclaiming their friendship, but would need to tread warily to resist stealing more.

"Thanks, but I need to get back to the squadron."

Chapter 6

She really needed to get back to work, but there were no new breaks in the investigation.

Nostalgia and longing mellowing her, Nikki stared down the empty corridor at the high school, only the rumblings of Saturday in-school suspension swelling from the lunchroom. At least she still had her tutoring stints here with older students until she resumed her junior high position. She glanced at her Minnie Mouse wristwatch she'd bought on a lark because she thought it would charm her cranky fourth period class.

Ten minutes early. Good. That would give her time to set up in the library.

Her footsteps echoed down the hall as she passed a poster announcing an FCA meeting. Good luck banners stretched for the basketball team along with a sign for the drama department's upcoming production of *The Lion, the Witch and the Wardrobe.*

She ached to teach her students, to recapture the rush of that moment when youthful eyes lit with enthusiasm over learning something new. She even loved the challenge of breaking through with the surly ones. Junior high was such a pivotal time, building foundations and confidence to carry into this high school world with temptations and dangers beyond any she'd seen just a few short years ago when she'd graduated.

And the world beyond was definitely scarier than she'd ever imagined.

Who'd have thought she would yearn for lesson plans? Or even a tour of bus duty? She would sacrifice almost anything for a stack of ungraded papers to take her mind off what happened in the yard with Carson. Had she really almost kissed him again? And why was he working so hard for her forgiveness now?

Nikki rounded the corner into the library where she would meet up with Billy Wade Watkins. The kid didn't seem particularly interested in learning, but he preferred school to home. A start. Hopefully he would realize that education was a means to a better life. Not that social services had been able to prove squat. He'd been removed and returned to his alcoholic parents twice over the years. She'd even tried to work some magic for the kid through the base since his father was retired military, but no luck.

She scanned rows of books lining the walls, more partitioning aisles and study stations until she spied the top of a masculine head in a computer booth, a dark-haired male like

Billy Wade, apparently making use of the free Internet time. She rounded a large circular table on her way to the cubicle. Feet came into view—no ratty Nike runners, but rather *leather loafers?*

Not the standard student gear around this school. So where was Billy Wade?

The male stood, Special Agent David Reis emerging from behind the cubicle wall. The last person she expected to see here, and one guaranteed to scare the bejesus out of her.

Her stomach bolted up to her throat. What was he doing *here?* And on a Saturday?

Willing her nerves to settle, she dropped her grade book, papers and text on the table to give herself an extra second to regain her composure around the investigator. Thank God he didn't have handcuffs in sight.

"Is there something I can help you with, Agent Reis? Did you receive the e-mail I sent to your office with a list of all Gary's friends?" Babbling. Not good, but she couldn't stop the tumble of words from her mouth. "I also forwarded a copy of the post Gary sent me that night, inviting me to join him at Beachcombers."

"I got it, but that's not what I'm here for." Reaching back behind the cube wall, he lifted a paper bag. "Here is your purse back. I'm sorry to say we have to keep your clothes for evidence."

And why bring it here? Unease tickled up her spine in spite of the lack of handcuffs. She took the sack grateful they'd let her have her credit cards and license that first day. Her clothes, however, they could keep forever. "I could have come to the base to pick it up."

"Thought I would save you the trip since I already had business out this way." He shoved his hands in his pockets, fished out a pack of gum, offering her a piece—she shook her head—before folding a stick in his mouth. All the while, he never took his eyes off her.

She resisted the urge to fidget like a bug under a science lab microscope. But wait? He already had business out here? "You've been questioning people I work with?"

"That bothers you?"

"Of course it does." She tossed the sack onto the round table with such force it slid to a stop against her grade book. "I've already been put on a leave of absence at the junior high because of this mess. I need my work back—"

"I'm sorry for any financial inconvenience."

His expressionless stare reminded her of a circling shark peering through that microscope, and sheesh what a mixed-up image that was. She really needed to air out her brain before she returned to work full-time.

And to do that, she needed to help Agent Reis however she could. "It's not about the money. It's about my students who need consistency. It's about how much I love my job."

"It's also about a man who lost his life."

"I understand that better than most, wouldn't you think?"

"Then you'll appreciate why I'm here." His shark stare warmed with a hint of human compassion. "Actually, coming here could well clear you."

"Clear me? Gary never came here."

"As I told your major friend when he came to my office, I have to consider that someone may have gone after Owens because of you."

As much as she wanted to rejoice over any option that cleared her, she cringed to think that she could have caused Gary's death, even inadvertently. "Who? I can hardly wrap my head around this."

"I can't discuss details of an ongoing investigation."

Even being a suspect brought such a total lack of privacy she felt exposed. Her hands twitched to check her sapphire button-down shirt with her black slacks. She hated the vulnerable gesture, the near irrepressible need to be sure she was totally covered.

She forced her hands back to her sides and hoped Reis hadn't noticed—only to realize the shark-eyed investigator hadn't missed a thing. In fact his gaze was still locked on her clothes.

On her body?

Okay, now she was totally feeling exposed and completely freaked out. He couldn't be interested in her. Could he?

He was an intriguing man, no doubt, handsome in a dark and serious kind of way. Which made him completely not her type since apparently she had a real weak spot for fair-headed charmers. But how did she discourage this guy without embarrassing both of them? Provided she was even reading him right.

Thank God Billy Wade Watkins chose that moment to amble through the library entrance, silver chains on his baggy clothes jangling. "Ms. Price? Sorry I'm late. I had to drop off my dad at some church meeting thing so I could use the truck."

"Over here, Billy Wade." She backed away from the investigator. "Agent Reis, thank you for bringing my things, but I have to get to work."

"Of course. Let me know if you remember anything more."
He leaned closer, his eyes over her shoulder. "Be careful.
Schools aren't the safest places to hang out these days."

He brushed around and past, leaving behind his Doublemint gum scent and unwelcome doubts about her students,
as well as questions about that whole strange once-over moment from Reis that still totally creeped her out. She'd been
so looking forward to this tutoring session, yet suddenly she
wanted nothing more than to rake pine straw with Carson.

And that unsettled her as much as the prospect of Reis prying in her personal life.

Prying the dog tag on his flight boot out of Jamie Price's
mouth, Carson passed the toddler a graham cracker in exchange. If only adults were as easy to figure out as the pint-
size versions. "There ya' go, kiddo."

The chubby-cheeked child snatched the treat and shoved
it into his mouth in a shower of crumbs and cuteness. Carson
ruffled the fella's dark curls, wiped the drool off the dog tag
and climbed back up the ladder in the Price kitchen to replace
the battery on the smoke detector.

He'd already checked every battery, furnace filter, window
and door lock, and still it wasn't enough. Nothing would be
enough until Nikki was in the clear and he knew exactly what
happened the night Gary Owens died.

So he worked to fix what he could.

After leaving Nikki and her too-tempting rake, he'd run
himself into a stupor until three in the morning. Not that sleep
came easy with her eyes haunting the back of his eyelids. By
sunrise, he'd decided his idea to spend more time with her

may have been ill-advised. He would return to his original plan to check in with her family and Reis.

Except halfway to the marina for a day of sailing, he'd turned toward her parents' place to ask her to join him—just to keep her occupied and cheer her up after her forced sabbatical. Right.

Wrong.

Jesus. He hadn't been led around by his libido like this since high school. Still he waited for Nikki rather than simply leaving. And actually, hanging out with her mama and short stuff wasn't a great hardship. He suspected there were a lot of clues to what made Nikki tick to be found in this ivy-stenciled kitchen.

Rena reached into the cabinet and pulled down two Mason jars like the others perched on her windowsill. Water and plant clippings filled each glass container, some stems sprouting new root webs. "You're really going above and beyond in your acting commander duties."

He folded the ladder and propped it beside the fridge.

"The squadron's only at half power with the rest deployed overseas." This house brimmed with so much life—plants, kid, pregnancy, even rising bread—he could hardly take it all in. *Take.* He hated that word and was trying his damnedest not to be a *taker* like his parents.

She twisted on the faucet and slid a jar underneath the gushing flow. "Even at half power, you're still dealing with quite a load if you're giving everyone this much individual attention."

Of course she would know better. He was doing his job and pulling overtime, but even that didn't involve multiple home visits in a week. "These are extraordinary circumstances. Besides, J.T. and I have history from crewing together. He would look out for my family in the same way—if I had one."

Out of smoke detectors and furnace filters to fix, he dropped his restless butt at the table. For years he'd never questioned his decision to stay single, but parked in this kitchen, he couldn't ignore the regret tugging at him as strongly as the toddler yanking on the dog tag on his boot again.

The water overflowed. "Do we have reason to worry about Nikki?"

He held out his hands to the little guy on the floor to buy himself time to think. Plunking the kid on his knee, Carson tugged the dog tags from around his neck and passed them over. "I wish I had the answer to that one, Rena, but I honestly don't know."

She shuffled the jar to the counter and filled the other, then tossed two fern clippings inside before placing them on the sill. "She only tells me the basics about what happened with Gary Owens, so I worry all the more."

"The OSI agent leading the investigation seems sharp."

Rena sank into a chair across from him, nudging a line of tiny Tonka trucks across the table toward her son who ignored them in favor of his new favorite teething toy—dog tags. "So the worst that could happen is that Nikki—" she paused, swallowed, then continued "—killed him in self-defense as opposed to an accidental death."

The worst? Someone could be gunning for her, far worse. And there were two women and a child here with just a college kid for protection. He didn't like this at all. To hell with worrying about treading warily while rebuilding a friendship. Damn straight he was concerned and he intended to talk to Reis about protection options. This would be easier if Rena and J. T. Price lived on base, except this whole mess had started on base. So if someone else had killed Owens, that someone had access to military installations.

All serious concerns, ones a pregnant woman didn't need. He studied her face as she rubbed her swelling belly.

"How are you feeling?"

She swung her feet up onto a spare chair. "Like I'll go stir-crazy sitting still for four more months."

"Seems to me there's plenty going on around here." He slid a discarded piece of junk mail across the table and started folding. "Don'tcha think, little guy?"

Jamie flashed him a gummy grin broken only by a few baby teeth and the remnants of graham cracker. Damn he was cute with all that dark hair and those saucer-wide dark eyes, in fact resembled the baby pictures of Nikki packing the house.

"You're good with children." Rena interrupted his thoughts.

Uh-oh. He knew that matchmaking tone well. He folded faster. "Uncle on-the-job training."

"You'll be a good father someday once you find that right woman."

He needed to put a stop to this line of conversation as quickly and politely as possible. He cranked a smile. "Why do all women assume a man's only single because he hasn't met the right woman?"

Her face pinked in sync with her embarrassed grimace.

"I'm sorry. That was presumptuous of me. Blame it on the inquisitive counselor not getting to log in those hours at work—" The phone chirped from the wall, interrupting whatever else she'd been planning to say.

Passing the kid the folded paper airplane to keep him quiet while Rena talked, Carson used the moment to gather his thoughts before the woman managed to wrench God-only-knew what else out of him. He definitely had too many secrets to let down his guard around her. He'd all but forgotten she was a shrink, she'd put him so at ease. Probably why she was reputed to be such a good one.

After the shoot-down and rescue in the Middle East, he'd been evaluated at a base in Germany. He'd managed to side-step the head examiners over there, a skill honed in his childhood.

Hindsight showed him his mistake. His alcoholism had flared after his return until he'd hooked up with A.A.

However sharing details in a therapeutic setting was totally different than spilling his guts to Rena Price. He was coming to terms with his childhood, but that didn't mean he wanted to take out a billboard about all his neglectful parents had forgotten to do for him and all the things their coked-up friends had tried to do *to* him. He couldn't understand how his sister managed to trust her genes enough to marry, much less procreate.

Procreate?

He could almost hear Nikki teasing him for his stuffy word choice. She was every bit as full of humor and life as this house.

Rena tucked the cordless phone under her chin and reached

for Jamie, clutching him close with an urgency that spoke of maternal fear. "I'll track down your brother to pick you up, sweetie."

Pick Nikki up? "What's wrong?"

She fished the paper airplane out of Jamie's mouth, hugging him tight again. "Nikki's stranded at the high school, car trouble."

Relief slammed through him. A simple spark plug or flooded car. Except wait. J. T. Price, a proficient mechanic, had taught his kids well. Premonition pricked a second before Rena continued.

"Someone slashed Nikki's tires."

Nikki kept her eyes on the access road leading into the high school parking lot, a preferable sight to her pitiful little truck with its deflated tires, currently being loaded on a flatbed tow truck.

Billy Wade shuffled from foot to foot, his baggy clothes defying gravity by staying on his body in spite of the weight of the mint of silver chains hanging off them. "Too bad we don't have four cans of that flat-fix-it stuff."

"It's okay, really. My ride's on the way. And honestly, I think my tires are beyond any can of foam repair."

"This really blows." Dyed black hair, long on one side, hung over his face in a greasy curtain. "When I find out who did this to you, he won't be bothering you no more."

"*Any*more. And thank you. That's sweet of you to worry, but once the school checks surveillance video footage, they'll probably be able to nail the person responsible."

He went stock-still. Too still. "They have cameras out here?"

"Yes, Billy Wade, they do." God, she hated suspecting him of doing anything illegal, but Reis's suspicions still rolled through her mind.

"I could, uh, just give you a ride, you know. My dad's truck might not look like much, but it runs real good and has four full tires."

"Your dad's truck looks a lot like my father's Ford."

"Really?" The teen's mask of bored insolence slid away for a rare second. "Your old man drives a beater, too? I wouldn'ta guessed we had anything in common."

He stepped closer. Too close. Into her personal space.

Okay, uncomfortable moment. Step back, keep her composure and take heart in knowing those surveillance cameras would show she hadn't made a single improper move with this kid. Although it saddened her heart that the days had long passed when a teacher could even pat a student on the back. A few pervs had ruined it for everyone else.

She crossed her arms over her chest. "Thank you for the offer, but I have a ride on the way."

"That him?" Billy Wade pointed to the turn lane.

And Carson's sparkling truck. That sure wasn't her brother behind the wheel.

Oh boy. Her mama was gonna have some explaining to do. Except that would necessitate showing how much it bothered her that Carson was the one picking her up instead of Chris, and in the middle of all those muddled emotions she was so darn relieved to see Carson driving their way. Four slashed tires, close on the heels of Agent Reis's warning really gave her the creeps.

"I can see why you'd rather go with him." Billy Wade's face returned to surly, a cover for insecurity—she was pretty sure.

The impulse to assert she and Carson were just friends bubbled up, then fizzed in light of better sense. Letting Billy Wade and any other boys around here think she and Carson were dating would work to her advantage. She wasn't much older than these students, so erecting boundaries was all the more important. "Thanks for hanging out to help."

"Sure. Whatever. Nothing else to do."

Billy Wade ambled over toward his father's rusted-out truck, chains on his saggy black pants jangling with each heavy step. He really was a sharp kid with a good heart, and a very real chance of landing in jail someday like his brothers.

Carson's truck shooshed to a stop beside her, hunky fly-boy behind the wheel in a navy-blue windbreaker for sailing and a smile that turned her heart over faster than that big cylinder engine of his.

"I hear you need a lift."

She turned her back on Billy Wade and the new host of worries she couldn't do anything about today.

Her eyes slid from Carson's chest to his scowl—directed right at Billy Wade as the teen continued his badass strut right past his truck and melded into the smoking cluster of other in-school-suspension students.

Nikki circled around to the passenger side and stepped up inside, supple leather warming her. Heated seats? An awesome feature she hadn't been able to afford in her little econo-truck currently on its way to a garage for a set of tires she was hard-pressed to finance. "You can wipe that disapproving look off your face."

Scowl showing no signs of fading, Carson eased his foot off the brake. "He's twice your size and a thug. This so-called 'look on my face' is totally justified."

"Appearances are deceiving." She instinctively defended her student as Carson drove from the lot. "He's a kid who's had a tough start and doesn't stand a chance at making anything of his life if he doesn't get extra help. It's frighteningly easy for a child with problems or special needs to go unnoticed."

He went silent at that for two traffic lights, stopped at the next before turning to her. "What happened to make him fall behind?"

"Dyslexia, which is especially tough to diagnose in a kid with a gifted IQ. He's smart, really smart, which helped him skate by for years with average grades. Add frequent military moves into the mix and it was easy for him to fall through the cracks."

"He's a genius with some kind of disability?"

"It's not as unlikely as you would think. One in three mentally gifted children has some kind of learning disability. The numbers could actually be higher since it's easy for schools to miss out on diagnosing the gifted dyslexic, especially when they're surprised a kid from his background is even passing at all."

"I wouldn't have thought about it that way. It sucks to think how many students could get lost in the system based on misconceptions."

He was being more insightful on the subject than she'd expected. Perhaps she'd been a little quick to judge him based on his silver-spoon background. "There are complexities to the levels and every dyslexic student is different. Basically, we figure out ways to send the information through another channel of the brain, usually a multisensory approach."

"For example?" he asked, seeming genuinely interested rather than merely making polite conversation.

That was more enticing than a surprise peek at his pecs. Well, almost.

"I have younger students trace spelling words in corn meal with a finger."

"Why not have all students do it that way? Sounds a helluva lot more fun than gripping a pencil until your fingers go numb."

"I agree."

He flashed a killer smile her way, sun reflecting off his aviator shades, darn near blinding her with the vibrancy. "Where were you when I was drilling spelling words? Wait." He thumped his head. "You weren't born yet."

"Are we beating that dead horse today?"

"With your vintage music fixation and my tapioca pudding, maybe we're not so far apart in age after all."

Something dangerous fluttered to life in her empty stomach. "Took you long enough to figure that one out."

"Too late, I'm guessing."

Was he regretting that? Hinting for something now? And sheesh, but she hated how even thinking it flipped her hungry stomach around. Not gonna go that route again. "Seems so."

"At least I can take comfort in knowing I'm not a COG."

"COG?"

"Creepy Old Guy."

Not by a long shot. She chewed the lip gloss off her suddenly aching lips. "Thanks for the ride and for showing up so soon, but where's Chris?"

"I was at your mother's when you called so I offered to come instead rather than waste time trying to track down your brother."

"Oh." That threw her for a second. Her stomach was in serious peril. "Uh, why? Anything wrong?"

"Nothing's wrong."

So why had he been there? She waited. And waited. "Thanks for coming out."

"Good thing, too. Probably didn't hurt for those students to see a man in your life."

"This is not your problem."

"I'm a male. I can't ignore it."

"I'm careful. I'm never alone with a student. Teachers are given training on just this subject for our protection and the students'. That's a part of why I always tutor on school property."

"All right. But I'm still picking you up until we find out what went on with Owens."

How silly to argue. She'd had the same concerns today. Her mother was confined to the house. Her brother was in and out of town visiting his girlfriend during college winter break.

And she couldn't hide from the truth. She wanted to be around Carson if for no other reason than to figure out a way to forget him as completely as she'd forgotten that night last week. "Since I don't have tires, I gratefully accept. For now."

"Thank you. And you'll be careful around that kid you're tutoring?"

Of course she would, but wondered at Carson's continued insistence. "You don't trust anyone, do you?"

"This isn't about me."

"I think it just became about you." She hitched a knee up to turn and face him even as he kept his eyes forward on the road. "You say you want to apologize, and sure you're help-ing. But I'm still confused. Can we only relate if things are about me? When does it become about you, too? Otherwise this is a one-sided, um, friendship—" yeah, friendship was a good word "—that's not fair to either of us."

His hands tightened around the wheel and she thought for a while he would simply keep driving until he whipped into the next turn. At a fast-food parking lot?

He threw the truck in park and turned to face her. "My par-ents were drug addicts."

Huh? That was a little more than she'd expected. She was thinking more along the lines of… What? She didn't know much of anything about him, and she wouldn't know more if she didn't unglue her tongue from the roof of her mouth and participate in this conversation. "I thought you said you had a privileged upbringing."

"I said my family has money."

"Guess I'm just as guilty of making character assumptions as you were with 'Thug.'" She couldn't stop herself from placing a sympathetic hand on his forearm. "I'm sorry—for the assumption and for how difficult your childhood must have been."

His quick nod offered his only acknowledgment of her em-pathy. With a brief squeeze of comfort she took her hand back, the heat of him tingling through her veins until she clenched her fist to hold on to the sensation. Already she could piece together parts he'd left unsaid, how no one thought to suspect anything, which left Carson and his sister unprotected.

Carson cut a quick glance over. "You can ease up a little on the sympathy. My sister and I went to great schools, and thank God for the nannies or things would have been a helluva lot worse."

"Somehow I think it was plenty bad enough." She shuffled this new image of Carson around in her mind and couldn't help but soften. "Where are your parents now?"

"Dad almost died of an overdose about two years ago." He recited the information in emotionless monotones. "Some thought that would scare him clean, he even tried. They've both been in and out of rehab clinics a dozen times and it never seemed to stick. Bottom line, I don't think either of them wants to change."

The resigned acceptance in his voice stabbed through her.

He kept his face forward even though their parking spot under the golden arches enabled him to look wherever he wished. "So, no. I don't trust easily."

Yet she couldn't miss how he'd trusted her today with a piece of himself and his past she suspected very few—if any—knew about.

"Enough heavy crap for one day." He reached for the door. "I hope burgers are okay."

"What?"

"Burgers. As in lunch, with some salty fries and a couple of apple pies. I assume you haven't eaten yet."

"No. But—"

"We'll get them to go."

"And where are we going with these burgers?"

He smiled. "Trust me."

God help her, she did.

Chapter 7

Trust was a tricky thing. Much easier to live up to than to give.

Carson parked his truck in the marina lot, more than a little humbled by how easily Nikki had gone along with his mystery plan. Although given the wariness creeping into her clear gray eyes as she looked across the line of bobbing boats down to Beachcombers Bar and Grill, she seemed ready to revoke her easy compliance.

"My sailboat's docked here now that I invested in something larger," he explained.

"Oh. Right. I thought for a minute you planned to wrangle some memories out of me and honestly, I've found that forcing it doesn't work." She sagged against the seat, staring out toward the bar with a melancholy weariness staining her eyes. "They always sneak up on me best when I'm not expecting anything."

"You're starting to remember what happened with Owens?"

She turned her head on the seat toward him. "Almost right away actually, I've gotten these smattering bits and pieces that may or may not be helpful. I shared everything with Agent Reis, for what it's worth. I even let Mom contact a hypnotist colleague from work, but I never could get past thinking what an ugly watch he was using for a focus point."

"Resistant?"

"Scared to death."

"Thank you for trusting me today." He wanted to say more, but knew better than to let things get any deeper and thereby ruin the afternoon. "Come on. I don't have lazy days much anymore and I intend to enjoy the hell out of this one."

Reaching into the back, he grabbed an extra windbreaker and tossed it to Nikki before snatching up their fast-food bags. Seemed she needed this day out on the water even more than he did. He couldn't help but think how in the past he would have offered a woman a more romantic meal such as croissants, fruit—mimosas.

Except he'd left behind his days of setting his mustache on fire with a flaming bar drink. His call sign Scorch may have stuck, but his party ways were long gone. He just hoped the burgers and sodas he had to offer now would be enough.

Even on the chilly winter day, the marina hummed with activity. No one swam in the frigid waters, but plenty perched on boat decks and along the docks wearing downy wind-breakers and cinched hoods, fishing off the pier or lounging on a bow. Carson searched the faces, wondering how many of them may have been at Beachcombers that night. Damn it, why couldn't he remember who he'd seen on his way to pick up his barbecue wings?

He'd been so hell-bent on getting out of there, the scent of whiskey and rum taking him to dangerous mental places. Then once he'd seen Nikki, he hadn't been looking at anyone else. He'd been tempted to hang out and talk to her as he'd done too often in the past. Since he'd been so tempted, he'd hauled ass away as fast as possible.

Guilt hammered him like the rogue swing of a boat boom. If he'd stayed around, maybe he could have prevented what happened. Owens would be alive. Nikki's life would be normal—and he would still be dodging her.

Wouldn't he? His fist tightened around the sack of burgers, which made him think of those brown-sugar-rich wings and that night all over again, not to mention another time he'd tasted hints of the sugary sauce while kissing Nikki after their friends' wedding.

Jesus, he really was in a crapload of trouble if he could remember who catered a wedding seven months ago. His feet thudded down the planked dock, past everything from a tiny Hobie catamaran manned by two teens in wet suits to a Beneteau yacht with jeweled partiers, toward his thirty-one-foot Catalina, a bargain bought used. Good thing boats didn't age like cars.

Without stopping, which would invite conversation and gossip, he waved at the crowded deck on the Dakota-Rat, a sailboat owned by Vic Jansen, the brother-in-law of fellow crew member Bo Rokowsky. The Rokowsky family outing resembled nothing from Carson's past but exactly the sort he'd wanted right down to the little blond kid with pigtails and a wife.

Except there was an empty space in the family since Bo was deployed.

Nikki shouted a greeting out over the water which would no doubt start the rumor mill churning at the squadron. He should have thought about that.

Maybe other people would have stepped in to help her if he hadn't preempted everyone else. Was he keeping her from something better on a personal level, too? She should have a houseful of children. She was a helluva teacher. He'd bet she would be an amazing mother, much like her own.

And she would. With some lucky bastard he didn't want to think about. Someday. Later. After he got her through this nightmarish time in her life safely.

"I brought you here to relax, but I didn't think about Beachcombers being so close. If it's a problem we can leave."

He stopped beside his boat slip, considering something else he could do to fill the day, kicking himself for assuming she would enjoy sailing as much as he did.

"No, really. It's all right. If I hid from every reminder of this whole mess, I would never go anywhere." She extended her hand. "Help me aboard?"

There she went again, being so trusting when he deserved to crawl for what he'd done. He certainly deserved more wariness. All he'd offered her were a couple of unsavory facts from his childhood.

He took her hand, a strong hand with short nails and impossibly soft skin he remembered, too. His memory flamed with their out-of-control kiss at his door, her hands tunneling up under his shirt, gliding her softness over him at a time when raw pain heated him from the inside out. He owed her so damn much.

Carson held her hand tighter as she stepped on the rocking hull, palmed her waist for the final boost. She looked so right there he wondered why he'd never thought to bring her before.

"Catch." He pitched the rope to her, leaped aboard and finished launching from the dock.

Already the familiar roll of the waves rocking beneath soothed his soul like a cradle in motion shooshes a baby. He took his place behind the wheel, firing the small motor to power them out of the narrow channel, Nikki an arm's reach away, trailing her fingers in the light spray.

She pulled her hand out. "Are you doing this today for my dad, too?"

"What part of trust me did you not understand?"

She flicked her damp fingers, showering an icy spray on his face. "Just joking."

Laughing, he leaned low and popped in the CD he'd bought this morning once he'd realized he would be detouring to her parents' house. He cranked the volume as the best of the 1940's spun up some "Bing" along with the percussion of the waves against the hull.

"Oh, you're playing dirty today."

"Gotta work with what you've got." He revved the motor to clear the channel without creating too large a wake to damage the shore.

The croon of the engine and slosh of waves mixed with Nikki's off-key croonings that somehow took on a musicality all their own.

After they finished the final bite of apple pie, she glanced over at him. "Thank you. This is really nice."

"I've missed running into you."

"Missed me showing up all the time, you mean?" She tipped her face into the sun. "God, I can hardly believe now how obvious I must have been with that mega embarrassing crush I had on you."

Had. Past tense.

Of course he'd known, and done his best to treat her like a little sister—except for one major lapse. He should have kept well away all the time, but God, she was charming.

He cut the motor, ready to switch to sail power. In a minute. After he had the answer to one more question he had to know now. "What do you think we would have done today if I hadn't screwed everything up then?"

"Hmm. You would have asked me to come along and I would have pretended it was no big deal. So we would have been doing the same thing, except now we're both coming into this with no expectations and being totally true to who we are. And speaking of being totally me, do you mind waiting a few more minutes to set sail?"

"Whatever works for you. This day is about you relaxing."

"Sometimes there's nothing more relaxing than getting your heart racing."

Heart racing? She couldn't actually mean what his body hoped she meant even if his mind knew better. She'd just said she was over her crush on him.

Before he could reason through the maze of her words, she'd jumped from her seat and clambered over to the main mast.

And up.

Holy crap.

Those long legs of hers in jeans and strong arms in his windbreaker shimmied her higher, her ponytail swaying from the back of her ball cap. He'd done the same countless times, but this was different. Enticingly different. He held the wheel and watched her stare out over the scenery, gasp in air, totally in the moment.

Sunlight streamed down over her. No makeup. No jewelry. But plenty of bling just from…her.

Bling and Bing. Modern but timeless, with a breezy sophistication in her old-soul self. He was toast.

So for the moment he surrendered and simply enjoyed the view of her slim body, the sweet curve of her bottom so perfectly on display. Sensory memory returned of gripping her taut roundness as he rolled her beneath him…

Who knew how much time he spent staring at her before she inched her way back down again and settled in a seat beside him. "Wow, the view from there is amazing."

Amazing. Yeah. That summed her up. "You scared the crap out of me, but that's one helluva pole dance, lady."

She threw her head back in her full-out laugh, so much more "real" than anything he could ever remember hearing or seeing in the affected world of his parents' social whirl. He raised the nylon sails, easing out the line bit by bit, savoring the increasing pull on his muscles.

Nikki shaded her eyes with her hand. "Do you need help?"

"I'll let you know. For now, just enjoy the ride."

Too bad he couldn't seem to take his own advice around this woman.

* * *

Her eyes full of sun, sail and sky, Nikki lounged along the cushioned seat while Carson manned the wheel like a Viking captain of old, making minor adjustments while the starburst-patterned nylon billowed. Why hadn't he named his boat? He obviously loved this vessel, and she could understand why.

Sailing offered a secluded slice of heaven.

He'd been right to bring her here. Tension from the investigation eased, even while another tension altogether kinked as she felt herself drawn in again by this man.

Except before, she never would have done something as impulsive and undignified as climb a mast while he could see her. How strange to realize that in those days she hadn't been true to herself. She hadn't shown him the total picture of Nikki Price. Or had she tried to morph herself into what she thought he wanted?

The craft picked up speed along the waves, biting through the wind like a plane cutting through the clouds. She imagined he looked much the same at the helm of his C-17. "If you love the water so much, why didn't you join the Navy?"

Feet planted and braced, his thigh muscles bulged against worn denim. "I didn't much like the idea of six months out on ship duty every year. Besides, the water's my hobby, my way of relaxing. If I turn it into work, I might lose that."

"Such as how I enjoy sports and running, but didn't want to be a gym teacher."

"Exactly." A gull winged low, dipping for supper in the

comfortable silence before he picked up the conversational thread again. "Have you sailed much?"

"Nope. This is my first time."

The wheel slithered through his shocked-slack fingers before he secured his grip again and redirected the bow. "You crawled up there blind? What if it hadn't been safe? Good God, haven't you pitched off enough high places into water for one month?"

His concern was more than a little touching. She brushed a reassuring hand over his thigh—whoa baby. She pulled her arm back. "You would have told me to stop."

"You're trusting me too easily."

"That's just my body, not my heart, pal. Two very different matters."

At least he had the grace to look away. "So this is your first boating trip."

"It's my first *sailing* outing, but I've been boating. My family camped a lot growing up. Dad had a little John boat." She'd forgotten about those outings until now, and took comfort from knowing her childhood hadn't been all about her parents' arguments. "He pulled it behind that old truck he still drives. I swear he'll be driving that same truck when he takes Jamie and the new baby off to college."

"Are you okay with these new additions to your family?" Alongside, a fish jumped and plopped.

"I'm a little old for sibling rivalry, don't you think?"

"Feelings aren't always reasonable."

She'd never even considered it, but searched her heart and came up with… "I feel more like their aunt than a sister, which makes me a little sad. But Mom and Dad are a lot stronger as a couple this go-round. The kids will have everything they need and more. Actually, since Dad's coming up on retirement in less than five years, he'll be pulling cupcake duty for elementary birthday parties while Mom works."

"Now that's an image guaranteed to spread grins around the squadron, a crusty old loadmaster stirring up a batch of frosting with sprinkles."

"I'll try to slip you some pictures."

His laugh rolled out over the cresting waves rippling toward one of the ka-jillion small historic battlefield parks throughout the Charleston area. "So you really are okay with the new rug rat siblings."

"Totally. They're gonna have a great life. Don't get me wrong, Chris and I had a good childhood in so many ways, but for these children, things will be more stable."

He set the autopilot and shifted to stand beside her, leaning back against the side. "So when your dad says no flyboys for his little girl, it's a sentiment you echo."

"That would be strange since I've spent so much time dating flyers." Was he only making idle conversation? Tough to think and decide with his body heat blasting.

"I figured it was a rebellion thing against your father."

No way was she confessing to her real reason for her recent run of flyboy dates who happened to have preppy blond good looks.

She shifted her attention to the boats in the distance and the ones remaining in the faraway dock by Beachcombers. More familiar memories of the place flooded her brain, stuffed fish peering down from over windows with glass eyeballs and slack jaws. Netting full of shells, sand dollars and coral stretched across the wall. Small lanterns rested on each wooden picnic table, the smoky blue glass letting little light flicker through, more mood setting than illuminating.

Nothing new, yet she still clung to every detail, searching for a hidden clue in the place where she'd run into Carson last week while waiting for Gary...

"Hey, babe," Gary's greeting jolted through Nikki a second before he leaned an elbow on the bar and kissed her neck.

She ducked to the side with the help of the spinning bar stool. "I was starting to wonder if you'd stood me up."

"Never." He tapped her nearly empty amaretto sour. "Could I get you another drink?"

The press of bodies stifled her. She wanted space. She wanted to go home.

But first she had to tell him what little relationship they'd had was over. "Two's my limit since I'm driving. I'll take some plain orange juice."

"You've got it." He angled over her shoulder to place the order, his chest sealing against her back until she could feel the imprint of his favorite belt buckle against her spine—a cold metal buckle shaped like an overlarge casino coin.

And the imprint of more steel, lower down.

Nikki hopped off the bar stool. "Let's find somewhere quiet to talk."

In public, but not right beside a table full of her father's fly buddies—Picasso, Mako and the new guy in the squadron, Avery, who she'd also dated a couple of times.

"Sure, just what I was thinking." Gary fell in step alongside her, then stopped, skimming a touch along her arm.

"Wait. You almost forgot your orange juice. Hold on and I'll go back and get your drink for you…"

"Nikki?" Carson's voice sliced through her memories like the hull slicing the waves.

"Yeah, uh right. Just daydreaming." Nikki clutched the side of the sailboat as if she could hold on to the memories already slipping away faster than the dispersing wake.

"Go right ahead." He shoved away from the side with muscle-rippling ease and a smile, closer. "This day's all about relaxing."

Even with the warmth of the sun on her face and her thick windbreaker protecting her from the misty spray, she rubbed her hands along her chilled arms, a deeper cold settling inside her at even the whisper of memory that helped her with nothing, except to hint further that Gary may have drugged her. He'd certainly had the opportunity. But hadn't she forgotten things from before he brought her drink? The effects of Rohypnol varied from person to person, with so many other variables factored in.

She searched her mind to recapture the faces that had been in the bar around her, all people she knew and simply accepted as part of her world. Why hadn't she paid more attention to details?

Okay, think. In addition to the crew sitting down for an after-flight meal, she'd seen Claire McDermott subbing for the bartender with her co-owner two sisters on hand waitressing. Hadn't one of them even dated Gary briefly? Which one?

She would call David Reis the minute she got home and tell him what little she could recall. Although he'd most certainly already interviewed everyone there that night, which made her feel exposed all over again, thinking of so many of her military friends knowing the details.

Damn it, she hadn't done anything wrong—that she knew of. She gave up recapturing the moment in the churning water and shifted her focus back to Carson, his face tipped upward to… Gauge the sail? The sun? Simply feel the wind?

She couldn't ignore the appeal of his strong features, the way his broad shoulders and lean hips turned her on and inside out all at once. What was it about him that called to her at a time when she shouldn't have been able to think about anything but the blind panic of clearing her name? He was good-looking, sure, in a preppy privileged kind of way that had never snagged her interest before she'd seen him for the first time and suddenly that had become her type for forever after, even if everyone else fell short.

As if sensing her stare, Carson looked down and over at her. His eyes narrowed. "What's with the frown, lady? Quit thinking so hard. Get back to your daydreaming."

She pulled a breezy salute. "Aye-aye, Major. Or would that be Captain since we're on your ship?"

"Either's fine as long as you smile."

Good advice, she knew. And wouldn't it be nice to settle into the circle of his arms, her back against his chest as they sailed the day away? Just the wind and sun and feel of his muscled chest.

Unbidden and unwelcome, a snippet from the memory flashed, of Gary's chest, that favored belt buckle of his biting into her spine….

Her mind hitched on the notion of Gary's belt, the one he'd been wearing the night he'd died. Or had he? She could swear there hadn't been a belt in his pants down around his ankles and she couldn't recall the security police having found one when they looked around the room while questioning her.

Blinking out of the fractured memory and into the streaming sunlight, she couldn't remember any more from that night. But she had one important question to answer.

Where was Gary's belt?

Chapter 8

Where was his head?

Sure as hell not in the job.

After a boring commander's lunch, Carson tossed his leather jacket over the brass anchor peg in his office on his last Monday as commander. The rest of the squadron was due back Friday and he could resume his regular job as the number two dude. He would be flying more again, but Nikki would have her dad back in town to check on her until Reis got his head out of his butt and figured out what happened to Owens.

And what would J.T. have to say about the time Carson had been spending with Nikki?

Their day sailing together had been good. Damn good, but he wanted to make sure he was a better man now so he didn't screw up his life again, or more importantly, didn't do anything to harm hers.

Tucking around his desk, he hooked a boot in the chair to roll it back while snagging a stack of performance reports off the top of his file cabinet. At least her memory was starting to trickle back. A missing belt wasn't much, yet remembering anything was a hopeful sign she might recall more. But if those memories revealed she'd killed Owens? Carson was certain she would have only done so in self-defense, which would put her in the clear legally.

All of which still didn't help him decide how to handle the next five days with Nikki.

He reached for the phone to check in with Reis about the security camera footage of the high school parking lot, only to be stopped short by a tap on the open office door. He glanced over to find Captain Nola Seabrook standing in the entryway. "What can I do for you?"

"Sir, I need to schedule a tactics class." The crisp blond officer stood at attention, even though Carson ran a more relaxed squadron than other commanders. "Is Wednesday at fourteen-hundred okay?"

"Wednesday?" He flipped though his day planner. "Uh… no. I've already scheduled confession for that time."

"Confession?"

"Flight safety meeting." He lapsed into his best Irish accent. "It's always better for the flyers to confess than have their sins pointed out by the bishop."

Laughing, she lost the starch in her spine. "Fair enough. How about we schedule the tactics meeting to follow when they're all softened up?"

"Roger." He nodded. "Spread the word."

Pivoting away, she ran smack into another person already

waiting. Seabrook laughed. "Guess we need to take a number to talk with the major today."

"Apparently so," answered his surprise visitor—Vic Jansen.

What was he doing here? Was it family business since his sister was married to one of the deployed flyers? Or personal, since Vic belonged to A.A., too.

Carson nodded to Seabrook. "That'll be all, Captain. And could you let my secretary know to hold calls for the next twenty minutes? Thanks."

Vic ducked into the room, a blond lumberjack-looking fella in flannel. The somber guy had lost his daughter in a drowning accident years ago, but recently started with the program because he feared he was reaching for a bottle too often.

"What brings you here?"

"Just dropping my sister off at the commissary. Since I had time to kill while she shops, I thought I would stop by, shoot the breeze if you have a free minute."

Carson rolled his office chair back an inch from the desk. "Sure," he said, even though he really didn't have twenty seconds to spare, much less twenty minutes. But something was obviously on Vic's mind and part of the program involved helping each other out. "What can I do for you?"

"Actually, I was wondering if everything's okay with you?" Jansen dropped into a seat across from the desk, blue eyes piercing.

The guy had seen him with Nikki yesterday, but that wouldn't be cause to ask if he was all right. Although pursuing this friendship with Nikki could well be termed insanity. "Why do you ask?"

"It's been a rough couple of months around the squadron with the extra duties overseas and now Owens's death," Jansen answered, his Dakota roots filling his rolling accent. "It's a tough time to be the king."

Ah, now the visit made sense. And damn, but the guy had a point. There weren't many people around this place Carson could talk to—none for that matter. But the A.A. bond of trust and confidentiality was a cornerstone. Solid.

"I could use some advice." The words fell out of his mouth.

"Hell, Carson, are you sure you want *my* advice? My track record sucks, don'tcha know." It was no secret that Jansen's wife had divorced him after the death of their daughter. But from what Carson could gather it sounded as if the woman's defection had been heartless, occurring before Jansen started drinking.

"I'll take any help I can get."

"Ah, so you want to romance Nikki Price."

"Who said we're talking about Nikki?"

"Last time I checked, they don't let morons graduate from veterinary school." The rugged large animal vet smirked.

Searching for the right words for thoughts he didn't even understand, he scooped up a miniature porthole clock from his desk and checked the battery, which of course was working just fine.

"Nikki and I have this—" tenacious attraction? "—bizarre friendship that seems to defy the whole twelve year age difference. I want to understand her."

"Good-freaking luck." Snorting, Vic hooked an ankle over his knee, work boot twitching. "If you figure women out, make sure you copyright the knowledge so you can retire a millionaire."

"I'm serious here." He thunked the tiny clock back on top of the stack of performance reports. "God, how do I explain this?"

"You like a woman as more than a friend, and she likes you back."

Might as well quit lying to everyone including himself. "So it seems."

"But the problem is…?"

"Problems. Plural. We tried things once before and I screwed it up." He ticked reasons off a finger at a time. "Her family would disapprove. I'm not sure I'm husband material and she definitely deserves it all."

"Whoa." Vic held up his work-scarred hands. "You're already using the M word. I thought you were talking about liking a woman and asking her out on a date. Don't you think you're jumping ahead of yourself?"

Didn't people date to see if something more would develop? And when a woman was obviously the happily-ever-after sort, wasn't it leading her on to date when he knew full well it wouldn't lead anywhere beyond a bed? Okay, so he was old-fashioned. He couldn't help it, probably went along with his tapioca pudding mentality.

"Did you apologize for what you did before, the time you screwed it up?"

He nodded.

"Have you done something to make up for it?"

Amends. A critical part of the twelve-step program, but also keeping in mind not to press for forgiveness if the action hurt that person worse. "I'm not sure I could make this one right."

"Did you try? Even if something can't be fixed, there's comfort in knowing the other person tried."

"I've been looking out for her, checking her security. Nikki's in a helluva vulnerable state."

"It must be tough for her to be so helpless."

"Nikki's a tough lady," Carson answered without even thinking—then stopped, the words and their truth kicking around in his head for a second before settling.

Why hadn't he realized it before? Sure Nikki had been dealt a raw deal right now, but he needed to stop viewing her as a victim. Had he done so as a convenient excuse to keep his distance?

He needed to quit thinking he was protecting her by ignoring the attraction, the connection. Not that he'd been all that successful. Relationships were a lot tougher to achieve than any Ivy League diploma on his wall.

Was he really considering asking her out on dates? Forget the age difference? Her father's objections. His own concerns about his ability to be an equal partner. A hefty dose of cons.

And only one reason in the pro column, a reason he couldn't even quite define. Something as nebulous as the way the wind in sails and the clouds against a windscreen soothed his soul. "You're right."

"Of course. No morons around here, remember?"

"We can only hope." He rocked back in his office chair. "Any suggestions for how I should make things right so I have a chance at moving forward?"

Jansen leaned forward, elbows on his knees. "There's no secret answer other than every woman is different. Quit trying to charge ahead with what you think she needs and just listen."

Another A.A. technique he should have figured out for himself.

Flipping his wrist to check his watch, Jansen winced. "I gotta make tracks." He shoved to his feet. "Give me a call anytime. Okay?"

"Will do."

Jansen paused by the door. "Hey, Carson?"

"What?"

"Good luck." The lumbering vet smirked.

"I'm going to need it figuring this lady out."

"That isn't what I meant." Jansen shook his head slowly. "I meant good luck, because Nikki Price's father is totally going to kick your officer ass."

Great. Just what every guy wanted to hear as he reached for the phone to call a woman.

Nikki strode along the wooden walkway toward Beachcombers chanting, "Idiot, idiot, idiot…" But a curiously excited idiot.

She'd looked forward to this outing since Carson called her yesterday and asked her to lunch. His invitation had quickly distracted her from the disappointment of learning the surveillance cameras at the school had been angled wrong to catch any helpful information about the vandalism to her little truck.

The planked path forked, one way snaking to the back bar and marina, the other route leading to the front entrance of the restaurant where she was *not* going on a date. Just meeting Carson at Beachcombers for a meal to help joggle more memories free. Regardless, thanks to a new set of tires on her Ranger providing transportation, she now stood outside Beachcombers.

She tromped up the steps to the sprawling wraparound porch that usually buzzed with conversation from the diners, but sported only sparse smokers in the cooler climate. Her stomach cramped with nerves, even more from the prospect of seeing Carson.

Pushing through the heavy door, she searched the crush of people in the wide hallway, a waiting area complete with gift shop stalls and cubbies. She weaved through the melee, the lunch crowd mirroring the weekend gang, but with a subdued workday air.

For the first time, she noticed the wide age range. She'd always been so focused on her friends—and yeah, the fly-boys—she hadn't noticed how many retirees frequented the place, as well. Were they around on the weekends, too? She would have to pay closer attention.

Flipping her wrist, she glanced at her Minnie Mouse watch. The second hand clicked past Minnie's glove.

Fifteen minutes early.

So much for appearing blasé. But she wasn't into game playing this go-round. She would be herself, totally—mast climbing, sarcophagus building, notoriously early Nikki Price.

Still no sign of Carson, but any number of crises at the squadron could have delayed him. She refused to turn into a quivering mass. He wouldn't be that important to her ever again.

Still, nerves whipped around in her stomach faster than

Minnie's second hand. Nikki fidgeted with the new gift shop items filling shelves along the waiting area walls—hand-painted T-shirts, seashell ornaments with Charleston's historic Rainbow Row inked in miniature. She mentally filed away craft ideas for her classroom during local history week. Her gaze settled on glazed sand dollars sporting a sticker of a C-17—the cargo plane flown by Carson.

Sheesh. Everything didn't have to be about Carson. Her dad and countless friends flew that same craft.

"May I help you with something?"

Nikki jolted and looked over her shoulder to find Beach-combers' proprietor, Claire McDermott. "Did you design these?"

Claire neatened the hanging racks of stenciled canvas bags in perfect descending order of largest to smallest. "My sister Starr did. I do most of the cooking, but we're short staffed out front today, so here I am. Our other sister handles the book-keeping." She straightened her apron on curvy hips Nikki had finally given up on ever developing by the end of high school. "It's a family effort we hope will pay off."

"From the crush today, it sure seems so."

No wonder Carson with his lack of family connection ate here so often, even moored his boat in the area. She wondered if that might be why he'd spent time with her before, because she came with a family. And man that sucked, wondering if you were liked because of your parents and brother. Or if he preferred curvy types like Claire.

Nikki stomped down feelings and thoughts that too closely resembled the insecure idiot she'd been over Carson months before. The present carried enough problems.

She could see the questions in Claire's eyes that she was too polite to ask about what happened a week ago. The woman had to be frustrated at even the least association with the scandal…yet the place was buzzing with activity. Sometimes bad press could be better for business than no press at all.

Claire's attention shifted beyond her. Bustling around the counter with brisk efficiency, she passed Nikki a pamphlet. "Here's a list of our upcoming performers in the bar, and don't miss the discount coupons on the bottom."

The woman disappeared into the milling customers, emerging on the other side near two men who seemed familiar…

Nikki shook her hands loose trying to relax for a memory to shimmer free. The shorter man wore a backward baseball cap and sports jersey. The other man loomed taller and burly in a plaid shirt.

The image gelled in her brain. Both men had met up with Carson that night out in the parking lot. Ball-cap dude, she didn't know. But the man in the plaid shirt was Bo Rokowsky's brother-in-law. What was the guy's name? Vic something-or-another.

A tingling started up her spine, a shift in the air, an awareness that Carson had arrived even though she hadn't seen him yet and no, no, no she didn't want that kind of surreal connection.

Maybe the feeling was—

There he was. Carson. Tall, slim and golden blond, his tan deep from a lifetime outside. She wished she could remember his tan line, but there had been covers by that point.

Whoops. Dangerous territory for her thoughts, especially in public. She glanced back up to his lean face, features angular and tense, phone pressed to his ear while he searched the crowd for…

Her.

Dimples creased—because of her. He nodded his hello from across the room as he continued to speak into his phone and make his way toward her. The tingle increased to an all-over body flush. Just a casual get-together?

She wasn't fooling anybody, most especially herself.

Only a fool would risk going out with this woman, but Carson had learned long ago, the word fit for him every time he came near Nikki.

Except he wouldn't sacrifice common sense and safety even though the whole meal had tempted him to toss both out the back hatch. At least they'd accomplished something at lunch, compiling a joint list of people they remembered Owens hanging out with, hoping they would recall something overlooked initially.

He'd insisted on following her home even though, yeah, she'd driven over on her own. Maybe he simply wanted their time together to last longer and it really wasn't that far out of his way. Lunch with her had been so natural and easy, too natural. In the past there had been the boundary of her crush, something that most definitely put him in an older man role. Now they met on more equal footing, even though she wore a Minnie Mouse watch that for some reason he found endearing as hell.

Slowing outside the Price home, he pulled up on the curb

behind her car, a perfect reminder of those slashed tires. No matter how tough and toned she appeared, she was still vulnerable to creeps who drugged drinks and tore her clothes.

The urge to protect pumped through his veins, thrummed in his ears, damn near blinding him. He could tell himself all day long to ease off the protector role because Nikki was strong, but in practice, she meant too much to him for him to be anywhere but by her side.

He blinked his vision clear and stepped from his truck just as she slid from hers, one slim leg at a time. Jeans never looked so good slung low on her slim hips, her jacket open to reveal a fuzzy sweater, bottom button undone to reveal a hint of skin.

Carson met her at her open truck door. "I'm sorry I was late for our lunch."

"You weren't late." She gripped the open door, Minnie Mouse waving from her wrist. "I was early, and I know things are insane at the squadron right now."

"Well, I wish I could have picked you up. Next time…"

Wind rustled pine needles from the trees overhead and lifted her hair while she chewed her lip and finally released the kissable fullness, slowly. "Next time."

There would be a next time.

Yes.

He covered her hand with his on the open door. "No new memories today?"

"Spotty stuff, mostly of when you and I talked." She scuffed her shoe through the dead grass, drawing his attention to her jean-clad legs—as if he needed an excuse. "I, uh, watched you walk away and meet up with two other guys."

Vic Jansen and Gary Owens's sponsor, on their way to a support meeting for families of addicts, not just alcoholics, but a catchall group. He couldn't tell her that, though, without breaking confidence. "Do you remember anything else?"

"Not really. It never works when I want it too much." Her gray eyes clouded, seeming wider when she didn't blink, just studied him until he wondered if they were still discussing lost hours a week ago.

"Then let's stop forcing the issue." He circled a finger along Minnie, then around to Nikki's wrist. "You said relaxing helps, so just let things happen."

Although a relaxed Nikki might be more temptation than he could handle.

"Okay, I have a question that's really been plaguing me." Her eyebrows pinched together with serious intensity that set him on edge.

"Sure, go ahead."

She tipped her head to the side, her hair teasing along his wrist. "Why haven't you named your boat yet?"

Tension rode out along his laugh. Relax. Right. Linking his fingers with hers, he slid their hands off the door into a true clasp rather than the sort-of-resting-here deal.

Tugging her forward, he reached past to close her door. "Naming a boat is like naming a new aviator."

"What do you mean?" She kept her hand in his.

Encouraging.

Arousing.

And so damn right he didn't let go.

"Well, for example, Lieutenant Avery is bucking for a call

sign to replace Bambi, but we've got to wait for the water-shed event."

"Like your flaming Dr Pepper moment when you scorched your mustache in a bar."

Now there was a splash of reality. "Exactly. A watershed event that sums up a person."

As if sensing his darkening mood, she stepped away even if she didn't release his hand. "I imagine you need to get back to the squadron."

"I've got another minute." He should have returned a half hour ago to tackle rewrites on performance reports and pro-motion recommendations, review and sign check-ride forms, all before the Wing Staff meeting at fifteen hundred.

He wasn't sure what he was doing standing here with Nikki. Even if he could see his way clear to risking a more serious relationship, he was scared spitless of marriage, and he couldn't even wrap his head around the whole father-kid deal. He could almost hear Vic Jansen laughing at him again since he kept gravitating right back to commitment thoughts.

One day at a time.

"Would you like to go boating again this weekend? Your dad will be home to look after your mom." And holy hell, he would somehow have to explain to J. T. Price why he was see-ing the man's daughter when the guy expressly didn't want flyboys for his baby girl. No doubt, Ivy League, officer fly-boys would fall even lower down the list for the practical val-ues of the crusty chief master sergeant.

Carson stroked his missing mustache. He would just have to get the guy alone and ease the news into the conversation.

They had a mutual respect for each other from shared crew experiences and POW hell.

"Boating?" Nikki asked, bringing him back to the moment.

Before he worried about talking to J.T., Nikki needed to agree.

"My plate will be clearer. We could moor up in a cove for lunch, maybe go ashore and backpack around for the day."

Her hand stilled, frozen like her blanked face. "Go boating to relax and take my mind off of Owens and my pathetic employment situation?"

"To spend time together. If that's okay."

Slack jawed for a painfully long second, she blinked fast. "Yeah, I think it is. As a matter of fact I'm sure it is." Her grin widened. "Although this time it's my turn to bring the food."

He liked the idea of her feeding him, him feeding her back, on the bow of his boat in the middle of the summer in a secluded bay where they could soak up the sun and each other....

Time to pull his mind off that fantasy, awesome though it was. And what was he doing having summer thoughts, months away? What had happened to taking things with Nikki one day at a time?

The rumble of an engine drew closer. Hair rose on the back of his neck. The neighborhood seemed sleepy and safe, but less than two years ago, Nikki's brother had a run-in with the law that brought threats from drug runners...a drive-by wreck and later a brick through the window.

He gripped Nikki's elbow. "I'll walk you to your door."

And check the security system for the umpteenth time.

The approaching vehicle slowed, a nondescript sedan. Carson hustled her faster up the walk. Once he got her inside, then he would deal with any problem, if there was one. The car stopped.

Agent Reis was behind the wheel.

What was he doing here? He couldn't be about to arrest her. No, no, and *hell no*.

The primal drive to protect—already on high alert—seared his nerves. He suppressed the urge to do more than tuck her away in the house. He burned to toss her in his truck and take her as far away as possible from any and every threat. God knew he had the money.

Nikki stepped around him and started down the walkway, toward Reis, so strong and resolute it damn near tore him up inside. She had a calm bravery under stress that would serve her well in combat.

He just prayed she wasn't about to enter the zone.

Reis tightened his tie, his coat flapping behind him as he charged up the curb. Sunglasses masked his expression, not that the man gave much away with full face showing. He extended a hand. "Major. Ms. Price. Glad I caught up with you so I can deliver some good news in person."

"Good news?" Carson pulled up behind Nikki, a palm to her back to brace her.

"Autopsy report finally came in, and Owens was definitely struck, and by a right-handed person. Since you're a lefty, that's good news for you. Even as fit as you are, it's unlikely you could have exerted such force with your right. While we haven't completely ruled anyone out, it's safe to say we're shifting our focus elsewhere for now. Although why that someone would want his belt…" He shrugged.

Nikki reached out to Carson, trembling a hint, her eyes still glued to Reis as he detailed more intricacies about the autopsy and height angles at the site of impact. Carson clasped her hand, a similar relief rocking him slam down to his feet. No one should have to carry the burden of having taken another life, even in self-defense.

Although since a large percentage of the world was right-handed, they hadn't narrowed the search much.

"I've already placed a call to your principal that you've been crossed off our suspect list. Given his sigh of relief, I imagine there's already a message waiting for you on your voice mail."

"Reis, I have to confess I'm not overly impressed with the protective drive-bys around here. A broken balcony, slashed tires, and all while she's being watched. Once word leaks that the investigation's no longer focused on Nikki, this person's going to get deadly serious in eliminating her before she remembers."

"I understand your concern, but we can't put someone in protective custody indefinitely." He chomped harder, faster on his gum. "But I've got connections downtown. I'll put some pressure on local police."

A fair offer, even if nothing short of a closed case seemed like enough now. "Thank you. And thanks for making the personal trip out."

"No problem. I need to ask her brother and mother some questions anyway, but I see now that their cars are gone. I should have called first."

Nikki's hand twitched clasped in his, but she stayed silent. "Have a nice afternoon, Major." Reis nodded. "Ms. Price."

Agent Reis slid into his nondescript blue sedan and pulled away from the curb. Once Reis's license plate disappeared around the corner, Carson hauled Nikki into his arms. "About time he figured out you couldn't have done something like that."

She trembled in his arms. "How could you be so sure?"

"I just knew, damn it." His arms convulsed tighter around her. "Although now there's not a chance you're going anywhere alone."

Nikki eased her head back to look up at him, not too far since she was tall, a perfect fit. "I'll worry about right-handed threats later. Right now, I'm so relieved at this sliver of hope."

"Fair enough. But I'm going to come back after work so we can all discuss more serious security."

Carson palmed the small of her back on the way up the side steps leading to the garage apartment. He scanned the single room efficiency, an open space with a futon, kitchenette and cubicle bathroom. Only one entrance in and out, with an alarm on the door as safe as she could be without him parking his butt with her 24/7, something she wouldn't allow anyway.

Although damn, what he wouldn't give for the pleasure of simply watching her sleep.

She slumped against the door frame. "Ohmigod, I knew I was stressed, but didn't even begin to know how much until now."

"You have reason to celebrate."

"Are you offering to celebrate with me?" Her loaded question broadsided him.

They were standing on the threshold of more than her apartment.

He cupped her face, fingers threading back into her loose hair. "What do you think?"

And somehow he was kissing her. He should pull away and make sure she wanted— Her lips parted under his and yeah. Just yeah. He tasted her and a hint of the barbecue they'd had for lunch.

Her hands skimmed along his back and up to loop around his neck. "No mustache," she murmured against his mouth. "Feels different."

"It's going to *be* different this time, too." His hands slid lower to cup her amazing bottom he'd admired as she climbed the mast. Hell, to be honest, he'd been checking her out since she'd strutted past him in shorts while subbing for a sick member of the squadron volleyball team.

All the reasons he should stay away faded under the onslaught of driving need to claim her as his, finally, totally, and damn it, memorize every second of the feel of her toned body under his hands because he wouldn't be idiot enough to treat her so recklessly again.

"Carson," Nikki whispered against his mouth, tugging him back to the present. "Either that's a phone ringing in your pocket or you're really happy to see me."

"Both." He dropped another quick kiss before pulling back. He fished out his cell phone, looked at the LCD panel and winced. "The squadron. I've got to take it." He flipped open his phone. "Hunt."

"Captain Seabrook. All hell's breaking loose here, sir. We need you back ASAP. There's been a bombing in the barracks overseas, the barracks housing our guys."

His gut burned raw with each forced even breath. He needed a status report. "SITREP?"

"One confirmed dead, more expected, but it's chaos there and here."

His gaze snapped straight to Nikki and her furrowing brow as she somehow picked up on his tension even though he'd kept his face neutral. Her father was over there along with so many of their friends, and there wasn't a thing he could do except be the bearer of the horrific details. With the taste of Nikki still on his lips, he was torn with the need to keep her close in case the news involved her.

But duty didn't give him that option.

"Hold down the fort. I'm on my way."

And he prayed when he came back to the Price home that it wouldn't be for an official notification visit.

Chapter 9

Six hours later, the phone rang on her mom's kitchen wall.

Slamming her memory journal shut, Nikki launched from her chair at the table to snatch up the cordless receiver and kicked herself for not placing it beside her, but she wasn't thinking clearly right now. Carson had told her there was a bombing overseas and to keep her pregnant mother away from the television until he could get details.

Please, God, let her father be all right.

And if her father wasn't okay, let her be strong enough when the time came to tell her mom. At least her mother was upstairs resting after supper, so Nikki would have time to pull herself together if the worst...

"Carson?" she gasped into the mouthpiece, her fingers numbing from her death grip. Death? Awful word choice. The smell of leftover spaghetti hanging in the air made her nauseous. "Is everything okay?"

Silence answered. A delay for a telemarketer recording? She glanced at the caller ID, which read "unknown" as she'd seen before when Carson used his cell.

She put the receiver to her ear again. "Carson? Is that you?"

Was the news so bad he was searching for the right words? But no. He was never that shaken. If anything, he became more focused in a crisis. She admired that about him, along with so many other traits she'd never noticed before, too caught up in her hormonal crush and a thousand other things that seemed frivolous now in light of how transient life could be.

Huffing breaths increased on the airwaves, sending a creepy chill down her spine. An obscene phone call? Or something far more sinister and dangerous?

Footsteps sounded from the living room, coming closer, loping—her brother.

"Hang up," Chris hissed, the television echoing Jamie's Disney flick from the other room.

"What?"

He yanked the phone from her and barked into the receiver, "The line's tapped, you bastard, so quit calling."

Chris nailed the off button and tossed the phone onto Jamie's empty high chair.

What was going on and why hadn't anyone bothered to tell her? "The phone's tapped?"

"We've been getting calls like that for two days, so Mom phoned that Agent Reis guy. Mom didn't want to scare you and since you stayed up in the garage apartment most of the time, you were never here when one came in."

Could that have been why Reis wanted to speak to her family?

And ohmigod, none of this even mattered if something had happened to her father.

Call, call, call. She touched the phone, willing it to ring with Carson on the other end. Her hand slid back to her side as she turned to her brother. "Were you going to tell me about the breather and speaking with Agent Reis?"

"Haven't had the chance since you've been so busy with your major squeeze." Her brother slouched against the counter with a leftover slice of garlic bread. "Major squeeze. Get it? He's a major?" When she didn't laugh, he frowned. "Is something wrong?"

No need for Chris to worry, too. Pulling a weak attempt at a smile, she pitched a pot holder at his head. "Major squeeze? That was pretty lame."

"So insult me or something. This is no fun if you won't fight back."

She dropped into a chair at the kitchen table, snitching up the cordless phone. "I'm just on edge." She nudged her memory journal aside, not that she'd been able to add anything to the blank page with worries for her father filling her head. "Now what about this mystery caller? What did Agent Reis have to say?"

The phone rang under her hand. She snatched it up, thumbing the on button, but wary of another call from "the breather." "Hello?"

"It's me." Carson.

She sighed her relief, only to have tension ratchet up all over again as she waited to hear what happened overseas.

"Your father's okay."

Thank God, Carson cut right to the chase. She grabbed the edge of the table to keep from falling off her seat, her whole body suddenly limp. Her silent, lumbering father would be coming home. She blinked back tears.

Chris frowned, starting toward her and reaching for the phone.

Nikki palmed the mouthpiece. "The call's for me."

"Sure, I can tell when I'm not wanted." He ambled back to the Disney flick, whispering "major squeeze" repeatedly. God, she loved her dorky brother who'd been so sweet helping out at home even after his classes resumed.

She slid her hand from the receiver. "I'm back. Sorry, but I wanted to send Chris out. Details? Please."

"Your dad wasn't even injured. I spoke with him a half hour ago." Carson rushed to reassure her. "I'm heading toward your house and I don't want your mother to freak out when I pull into the driveway."

"She's upstairs resting."

"Good," he answered, his voice so…dead? "Are you free?"

What did he need to say that couldn't be relayed over the phone? "Just hanging out with Chris and Jamie, watching *Jungle Book.*"

"Could you explain to Chris what's going on so he can tell your mom if she wakes up and there's something on the news?"

"Sure, but do you really think there will be anything on TV?"

"It was bad over there, Nikki." Cell phone static echoed along with the silence and what sounded like a heavy swallow. "I'm pulling into the driveway now. Could you meet me outside?"

He was upset. Of course he was. And oh God, he'd come to her.

"Give me thirty seconds to update Chris, and then I'm out the door."

"Thank you."

His bass rumbled even deeper, hoarse with emotion. If the accident didn't involve her father, there could only be one reason Carson had driven over.

He needed her. A couple of weeks ago she would have expected to take satisfaction from that. Now, she could only think of racing out the door, her heart as heavy as his voice over the phone at just the thought of him being in pain.

Studying the tops of his flight boots, Carson slumped against his truck tailgate, not sure why he'd driven here, but knowing if he didn't he might land in the bottom of a bottle before morning.

Even though he'd wanted to run to Nikki from the start, he'd tried to find his sponsor. Nikki shouldn't have to deal with his crap. But his sponsor hadn't been at home or at work or even picking up his cell phone.

Streetlights flickered on, doing little to brighten his mood. He needed to stop thinking about the past hours spent informing a woman her husband wasn't coming home. Of more hours telling two other women their husbands were being flown to Germany for surgery and God only knew if they would survive.

Still checking out his boots and that lone dog tag attached to ID a dead aviator when his body was blown to bits, Carson heard the front door creak open and bang closed. Nikki's footsteps—he was too tired to question how he knew it was her without even looking—thudded down the porch stairs. Closer, until her gym shoes and the hem of her jeans appeared in view.

He looked up and let himself soak in the sight of her makeup-free face, hair straggling from her haphazard ponytail. He'd been right to come here.

Carson fished out his keys and passed them to her. "Feel like driving? I even brought along your CD."

"Sure. Who would turn down the chance to drive a great new machine like this?" She took the keys from his hand, lingering for a quick comforting second before pulling away as if sensing he couldn't take too much emotion.

Without another word—and God bless her, no questions, yet—she slid behind the wheel, cranked the engine and rolled down the windows.

She handled the vehicle with her typical confidence, so he relaxed, only as his eyes slid closed realizing he never sat in the passenger seat. Even in the plane, he was the aircraft commander. His copilot days were long past.

Having an equal partner was rare.

He homed in on sounds to blot out thoughts—cars roaring past, the road reverberation shifting in tune as they ascended a bridge. A barge chugged in the distance, a long mournful horn echoing.

Inhale. Exhale. Forget. Inhale beach air. Salt water. Marsh. The scent of Nikki's soap. He was being selfish making her wait.

He turned his head along the seat. "I guess you want to know what happened."

"You'll tell me when you're ready." She kept her eyes forward, hands at ten and two, a rock when he needed one so damned much.

"I'm ready to talk whenever you want to pull over."

"Okay then. I know a quiet place not too far from here." A few miles later, she took the next exit off the highway, down a two-lane road along the shore, finally turning onto a dirt road leading to a tiny deserted historical landmark. The small battlefield boasted little more than a couple of minicannons, a broken cement bench and a sign explaining what happened here over two hundred and twenty-five years ago.

Shutting off the engine, Nikki shifted in the seat, leather creaking. "How about we sit in the back of the truck and look at the stars?"

She understood him so well it shook him sometimes since he didn't much like people rooting around in the cobweb-filled darkness of his head.

Well damn. Could that have been a part of why he'd run so hard and fast in the other direction after waking up in her bed? Not a reassuring thought in the least since he'd always told himself he stayed away for her, rather than risk hurting her again.

He leaned over to the backseat and pulled a bedroll of blankets forward. "I sleep outside sometimes."

In the back of his truck or the deck of his boat, the solitude and stars called to him. Except tonight he needed Nikki beside him.

Carson turned the key to keep the CD playing, windows

down before he stepped outside and dropped the back hatch. He unrolled the bedding, tossing the sleeping bag for cushion and shaking out the extra blanket to wrap around them, trying like crazy to ignore the intimacy of the whole action.

The night wasn't that cold, high forties maybe, with a bit of a bite in the crisp air. He followed her into the truck bed, sitting beside her, draping the blanket over their shoulders, their legs stretched out side by side with a tree bower overhead. A few stars twinkled through, but the overall haven effect blocked out the world.

By instinct, he slid his arm around her waist and she didn't object, simply tucked her head on his shoulder while they both leaned against the cab and stared up at the sky. The time had come to talk. As much as he hated pouring out the horror of the day at her feet, here they were, and he was learning Nikki was a lot stronger than he'd known.

"There was a bombing at the barracks housing our crews. Two injured." His head thunked back against the glass. "One dead."

Her hand fell to his thigh in a steady weight of comfort. "Who died?"

"The young loadmaster, Gabby." So named "Gabby" because the kid talked all the time and now would never speak again. "I had to tell his wife. She's only twenty years old, Nikki. Twenty damn years old and already a widow."

Her fingers squeezed tight on his thigh. She stayed silent. What could she say anyway? There weren't words for this. God knew he'd looked for them when speaking to Gabby's wife, and he'd said *something,* undoubtedly inadequate. He'd taken flight surgeon Monica Korba and Chaplain Murdoch with him, but ultimately telling her was his responsibility, his squadron, his lost wingman.

Big band tunes from WWII teased from the truck cab, the pair of chipped cannons leaning. Symbols of so much loss.

"I don't know how the commanders during World War II handled all the deaths." His chin fell to rest on top of her head, the scent of her mingling with the ocean air to fill the hollowness inside him.

"You said two were injured?"

This had to be traumatic for her, too. These people were her friends. He cupped her shoulder and hugged her closer. "Bronco and Joker."

She gasped, just a slight hitch she swallowed back without looking up at him.

He rubbed her arm until her breathing settled again. "Bronco was pinned by a beam when the barracks collapsed. He's got a few crushed ribs and a punctured lung. Joker caught flying glass in the chest and face. I spoke to Joker's fiancée right before she was supposed to leave for work. She kept trying to find her shoes as if that would make everything all right."

Her arms slipped around his waist and she held tight, offering a comfort he wouldn't ask for but was grateful she thought to give.

He forced down the acrid taste in his mouth insidiously whispering for a shot of something smooth to wash it away. "We finally caught up with Bronco's wife. Since she's a military doc she kept trying to discuss everything in medical terms with Doc Korba, but her hands and voice were shaking so bad while she talked… Bronco's little girl was running around the living room like everything was fine and she didn't have a clue her daddy's on an operating table in another country."

His voice cracked. Damn it. He scrubbed his hand under his nose and started to stand. "We should go back now."

She reached up, clasped his hand and stopped him. "Do you have to return to the squadron?"

"No. There's nothing more I can do tonight." He looked down at her, her old-time music riding the breeze, moonlight streaming silver glints in her hair with a timeless hint of what she might look like in thirty years.

Nikki tugged. "Then let's stay here."

"I'm pretty messed up in the head and we both know what happens when I can't think straight around you."

"Have you been drinking?"

"No." He wanted to, but was hanging on now, thanks to her.

"Neither have I." She tugged again. "Stay. Let's look at the stars and talk if we need to or just be quiet. But I don't think either of us is ready to go back yet."

He knelt beside her. "How did you get so smart so young?"

"It's in the music."

He knew better.

The age difference excuses weren't going to work for him anymore. While there were certainly a legion of other problems they would have to deal with later, for tonight at least they were both on even footing and in need of something they could only find together.

Cradling her face in his hands, Carson gave up the fight and kissed her.

* * *

Nikki didn't even think of pulling away from Carson and the warm pressure of his mouth against hers. In fact, she didn't expect to pull away from him at all for a long time tonight.

Halfway through his outpouring about speaking with the families, her heart had softened the rest of the way toward forgiving him for what happened before. Any man who noticed the vulnerability in a woman spinning circles to find her shoes in a crisis…well, that man had a deep and tender heart.

She wasn't sure what she intended to do with him after tonight, but she would never be able to move forward if she didn't finish what they'd started months ago. What better place to be together than out in the open? Away from the world that seemed to intrude too often and insist they were wrong for each other, for a litany of reasons she couldn't remember because the bold sweep of his tongue stole every thought right out of her head.

What was it about him? Could it simply be his experience that made men her age seem like boys? He certainly did know his way around a nerve-humming kiss that made her forget the nip in the air. In fact she could swear her skin was steaming as hotly as the blood coursing through her veins. His palm sketched along her stomach, bared as her sweater hitched, the bottom button already open in a V.

Arching—was that a purr coming from her?—she savored his calluses gained from years sailing, the gentle rasp a tantalizing abrasion against her oversensitive skin. She wanted more, more kisses, touch, sensation.

Everything, here under the bower of trees and light of a harvest moon glinting on the water.

He leaned forward, or she angled down, or they both simply followed gravity to the sleeping bag. She wasn't sure and didn't care as long as they both were flat. Soon. Yes. She sank into the giving softness, his body blanketing hers while he braced on his elbows to keep his weight off her.

Her legs locked around his at the knees, her hands urging against his rippling shoulders. "I want it all tonight."

No half measures like their other time together.

Still he kept the full press of himself off her, the sleeping bag only offering so much protection from the steel truck bed. He peered down at her, blue eyes deepening to a midnight hue almost as dark as the sky. "Things are moving fast here tonight. Are you sure this is what you want?"

"Do you plan to walk out on me afterward?"

"I tried to stay away and we saw how well that worked for me. I've thought about you every damn second for seven months."

"Good." Nice to know she hadn't suffered this alone.

"So there's a vindictive streak in you after all." His mouth creased up in a smile she burned to explore with the tip of her tongue. "I was wondering how you could forgive me so easily when you're well within your right to be kicking my ass into eternity for what I did."

"Actually, I think I owe you an apology, as well, for what happened then. I knew you weren't in any shape to make an important decision like going to bed together."

It felt good to finally voice the guilt she'd been hiding for months. As much as his walking away had hurt her, it was about time she accepted her own role.

He flipped to his side, palming the bared patch of skin

above her low-riding jeans. "While I still think any culpability rests squarely on my shoulders, we can start clean tonight."

She liked the sound of that. "Does that mean we're back to a first date? Because I won't go to bed with a guy on a first date."

His hand tunneled a hint higher up her sweater. "How about a clean slate with a history of friendship and dates."

"Sounds good to me." Especially if he would keep stroking her rib cage.

He thumbed the underside of her breast, teasing the swell through satin. "Right now I wouldn't mind hearing exactly what you want."

"I want to be with you." She slid the top button free from her lemon-yellow sweater, cool breeze drifting along passion-heated flesh.

His blue eyes lit with shock—and desire. "Uh, I meant back at my place, or yours."

"What's wrong with here?"

A growl rumbled low in his chest, vibrating against hers. "Not a damn thing."

He tracked her hands, freeing button after button until her sweater parted. She wondered at her own boldness for an instant, then gloried in it as his gaze hooked on her breasts. The chill in the air puckered her nipples tight against the scant satin and lace.

His pupils widened with increasing passion. As if she couldn't already feel the evidence of his growing arousal throbbing against her.

She reached for the front clasp of her bra, and thank goodness she'd put on the good stuff this morning, pale yellow Victoria's Secret. On sale. And holy cow she was rambling in her brain to ward off embarrassment.

The cold kissed her skin a second before his mouth. Moist heat flowed from him through her veins until she longed to shrug away the heavy blanket, but her languid body wouldn't obey commands from her brain. Only instinct. Her frantic hands grappled over Carson, hungry to touch as much of him as possible after yearning for so damn long. Much more and she would combust.

His hands slid lower to her bottom, drawing her nearer. They rolled along the truck bed in a tangle of arms and legs that should have hurt but sensation suffused her to the exclusion of anything else.

Cocooned in the blanket, she kicked free of her jeans, needing to be rid of the confining clothes. Her sweater hung from her shoulders as her bare breasts brushed along the rough fabric of his flight suit as they lay side by side.

The flight suit unzipped from the bottom for easy access during flight, and she definitely intended for them both to fly now, with the sky and stars, sound of the waves in her ears, the best of both worlds.

"Birth control?" she mumbled against his mouth.

"In my wallet." He combed his hands deeper through her hair, holding her with an intensity that rocked her. "Nikki, I swear I'm going to be around after."

"Can we talk about that later?" She only wanted to focus on finally feeling all of him all over her.

"I'm just doing my damnedest to be honorable here."

One of the things she admired about him, but right now

he'd turned her inside out until she couldn't have run enough miles to burn off the frenetic energy zinging through her.

"It would be very dishonorable to leave me unsatisfied." Stretched beside him, she wrapped her fingers around the thick length of him, learning the silken steel texture of him. His groan thrilled her as much as his touch, knowing *she* brought him pleasure. She suspected the timeless tunes from the stereo would arouse her mercilessly from now on.

He tugged out his wallet, pulled free a tiny packet and sheathed himself with a speed that spoke of an urgency echoed inside her.

Hooking his hand behind her knee, he hitched her leg higher, over his hip until she realized what he intended. No missionary position tonight. Fair enough. She liked the idea of taking this journey side by side.

Then the thick blunt prodding stopped her thoughts altogether as she focused on this moment she knew would change things between them forever. Deeper, deeper still, she took him inside her body and more, slowly, carefully, staring into his eyes and soul in a way she never had months ago when she'd been too wrapped up in her hero worship to see the man.

She winced at the uncomfortable pinch and stretch, settled, waited for her body to adjust around him.

"Okay?" he asked, his jaw flexing from a restraint he couldn't hide.

"Totally." She rocked against him once, twice, again, his grip on her hips helping her find a matching rhythm of their bodies together. Moving. Rocking to increase the pleasure of his slick thrusts.

He shifted onto his back, holding her in place during the

shuffle, the blanket slithering down around her waist, her sweater flapping open while he laved attention over her breasts.

His hand slid between them, touching where their bodies met, circling in time with her writhing hips against him. Her womb clenched tight, tighter, as tight as her legs clamping him to her as she chased the release so close… closer…

Waves of pleasure sluiced over her, pulsing like the breakers gushing against the shore, then receding slowly and stealing her muscles from her body until she slumped on top of him. Two deep thrusts later, his arms convulsed around her in time with his hoarse growl of completion.

Slowly, her senses tuned back in on things other than the residual pleasure pulsing through her.

Waves surged and crashed while the stereo piped one of her favorite songs, "Don't Sit Under the Apple Tree." Now she knew why.

Nikki grinned against his neck, tasting the sweat on his skin. "After all our talk about being old and mature, here we are in the back of a truck."

His hands roved up and down her spine. "I've never made love in the back of a truck."

"Me, either." Nor had she made love anywhere else for that matter.

A fact she now knew for certain.

She'd been almost sure nothing happened with Gary. The doctor in the emergency room had reassured her there were no signs of penetration, and she'd believed intellectually, but her mind had felt so violated it had been difficult to look beyond that. Now at least she had physical reassurance that she had not slept with Gary Owens—or any man for that matter.

Because making love in the back of a truck had been a first for her in more ways than one.

Chapter 10

Nikki was a virgin.

Past tense now.

Carson still couldn't wrap his brain around the fact, even as they sprawled in bed—at her apartment, not the garage place at her parents. After they'd untangled themselves from the sleeping bag in the back of his truck, he'd hesitated to take her to his house because of the bad memories it might hold for her, so he'd suggested her empty apartment. Since it was now common knowledge she'd moved out, there was no reason to fear hanging out in the place for a few hours.

An arm tucked under his head, the other curved around Nikki while she slept curled against his side, he stared up at her ceiling fan clicking overhead, circulating the heat. A tiny soccer ball dangled from the chain, spinning lazy rings in the air. Her room surprised him. She was such a no frills and leanly honed person he hadn't expected something so...frou-frou. From her ruffly curtains to the poufy spread, patterned with tiny pink flowers and little green leaves.

Then there was that soccer ball chain pull overhead.

The dichotomy was somehow so totally Nikki the image settled in his brain as he grew even closer to this woman he'd fought hard to resist. How many other facets to her personality had he missed because of preconceived notions?

And the biggest mistaken notion of all... Damn it, he should have figured out she'd never made love *before* he came up against the hint of a barrier. Which shocked the hell out of him.

Although she was a quick study.

Still, if he'd known he would have...what? Turned away? Probably not, but at least he could have offered her a gentler, more romantic first time. Being with her blew his mind beyond anything he'd ever experienced. He knew now there wasn't a chance he could have been with her seven months ago and forgotten.

However now he wondered what *had* happened between them. When he reexamined their conversations about that night, never once did she say they had sex, only that they'd gone to his place. Not that they'd discussed it much—his own damn fault.

He remembered waking up naked together, so they must have gotten mighty damn close before he passed out. God. He owed her an even bigger apology than he'd thought.

Nikki stirred against his side and sighed over his chest before pressing a kiss to his shoulder, stirring a *good morning* down south even in the middle of the night. He willed away the erection—okay, it wasn't going down any time soon, but at least he reined himself in and simply rolled toward her for a simple kiss.

Simple? Not for long.

Carson sailed his hand along her naked spine. "You're awake."

Her fingers skipped down his chest. Lower. Gliding one finger from tip to base. "So are you."

He clamped a hand around her wrist. "As much as I would really enjoy an encore, again, you need more time to recover."

"Women don't have a recovery time like guys."

"That's not what I meant." He pressed a kiss to the palm of her hand and resisted the urge to taste more instead of talking about what promised to be a sticky subject. "You were still a virgin."

She stilled for six clicks of the ceiling fan overhead before flipping to her back, sheet clutched to her creamy chest. "I was wondering if you noticed that little fact."

Tough to miss. Just the memory of her tight heat had him throbbing all over again.

While he couldn't have all of her just yet, he allowed himself the pleasure of teasing her tangled hair along the pillow and rubbing a dark lock between two fingers. "Twice tonight was probably already one more time than was wise for your body. Tomorrow, though, I'll be more than happy to take you up on that offer."

"So we're done for tonight?"

Her obvious disappointment stirred him as much as any touch. If she was game, he had a few ideas of how they could spend the remaining hours before sunrise and a return to the real world. "Unless I can interest you in a bath?"

"A bath?" She sat up, flowered sheet slithering down to pool around her waist while she studied him with unabashed enthusiasm.

Forget oysters, this woman was a walking, talking, living, breathing aphrodisiac.

"A steaming bath would be good for all those new muscles you used tonight." He swung his feet from the bed and held out a hand for her.

Linking their fingers, she followed him into the bathroom, leaning to twist on the water—and whoa what a view. Passion fogged his vision.

Steady.

Stepping over her seashell-shaped bath mat, he lowered himself into the tub, then settled her in front of him while the faucet sluiced steaming water over their feet, her sweet bottom pressing a soft torment against him. Way to go, genius.

His skull was going to explode before he could get around to discussing the pink elephant looming in the middle of her ocean-themed bathroom. "I thought we had sex seven months ago."

Arms draped along the sides of the tub, she tipped her head on his shoulder to look at him, surprise sparkling in her crystal-gray eyes. "You don't remember what happened that night? I think you owe me a new apology."

Ah hell. Not a pink elephant at all for her, since she didn't have a clue what he'd thought.

This really was screwed up and now he'd made it worse. He needed to unscramble his brain to get through this, tough to do when his eyes were full of Nikki's legs…and more. "What did you think I was apologizing for last week?"

"For passing out on top of me seconds before the act." Pink tinged her cheeks, but he suspected it had nothing to do with the steam rising from the water around them. "And I figured you were apologizing most of all for walking out the next morning and never calling."

"That last part, absolutely. The first part, God yes, I'm apologizing for that now, as well. I'm sorry for being in no shape to ask you to stay the night with me and for being selfish enough to do it anyway."

"I can't believe that for all these months you thought we slept together." Confusion smoked through her eyes. "At least you're off the hook for that."

"Not even close. Doesn't matter that my body shut down, the intent to make love to you remained even though I knew I should stay away." He rested his chin on her head, remembering enough of that night to know that nothing, nothing was more important to him then than being with Nikki. And that unsettled the hell out of him because he still felt the same.

"Maybe you would have had second thoughts if you hadn't passed out."

"I doubt it. I'd wanted to be with you for so damn long." Which brought them back to the present. "And here we are again."

"Except things went better this time." Her smile granted forgiveness he still wasn't sure he deserved.

"I want afterward to be better, too." He clasped her hands in his, linking them over her stomach.

"Although I can't image how the 'during' part could be any better."

His thumbs brushed along the soft undersides of her breasts, perspiration from the heated water dotting her chest and begging him to taste her. "I would take that as a compliment, but you had twenty-three years of buildup going."

"Who says I went totally without for twenty-three years?" Pure sensuality emanated from her smile. "I'm a woman who can take care of herself."

He choked on a cough. *Take care of herself?* She couldn't mean… He searched deeper into her narrowed eyes and holy crap, she most definitely meant exactly what he thought.

Carson linked their fingers tighter, holding hands as much touching as he could risk with his body on fire from just her words. "Now there's an image I could enjoy for a damn long time."

Nikki's smile widened and she guided one of his hands down her belly, dipping deeper into the water. "Or you could enjoy it along with me now for real."

His brain went on stun, then revved to life because no way was he missing out on a second of this fantasy come to life.

Nikki reclined back against his chest, her knees parting in the move of an awesomely bold innocent. She guided his hand lower, her hand over his cupping the core of her.

She brought their other fisted hands up over her breast, unfurling her fingers until she flatted his palm to her pebbled peak. Slowly she guided his hand along her skin, her impossibly tight nipple tightening further. He swallowed hard.

Her mouth tipped in a slight smile. She couldn't miss the sway she held over him and damned if he cared about his surrender so long as she continued to lead his touch, growing bolder as her pupils widened with unmistakable pleasure.

He throbbed harder against the sweet press of her bottom.

Her other hand, underwater over his, twitched, tangling his fingers in short dark curls, dipping into moist heat and rubbing slow circles with his fingers against the hidden bud beading as tight and hard as her nipple minutes before.

Much more of this and he would explode. He started to pull his hand away and she held him firm, her breathing faster, her heart hammering so hard he could feel it through her back against his chest…until her spine bowed forward in time with her gasp, another, then a low moaning exhale as she sagged against him again, a limp, soft weight.

He soothed her through the aftershocks with steady pressure, whispering in her ear, "Definitely an image to carry with me. You're one helluva woman, Nikki Price."

Her head lolling, she nuzzled his shoulder. "While I can take care of myself, I've found it's all the better with you along."

Tomorrow, he would take her up on that. For now, he held her while the water chilled around them, reminding him of the cold reality.

He was fast losing control of his feelings for this complicated woman.

So much for believing she could keep things uncomplicated with Carson.

Stretching her leg to toe on the faucet to reheat the bath, she couldn't decide whether to be totally mortified by what they'd just done or simply languish in the afterglow and warming water. Sheesh, when she decided to let down her boundaries, she really went all the way. "You were totally right about a bath relaxing me."

His light laugh ruffled her hair, uneasiness seeping from her toes.

Carson's arms tightened, their hands linked over her stomach. "Thank you for trusting me to be your first."

"You're welcome." Definitely not simple anymore. From the minute she'd met him, she'd wanted him to be her first.

Her last?

"Do you mind if I ask why you waited so long?" He stretched his foot to turn off the water.

He'd shared so much about himself and his growing-up years, it seemed selfish to hold back, especially when her past was so much less traumatic than his. "My parents had to get married when my mom was only eighteen. Mom was already pregnant with me. It's not something we discussed, but I always wondered if they fought because of me."

"You know better now, right?"

Sort of. "Chris told me he brought up my 'premature' birth once and Dad almost decked him."

"Since your father's one of the least violent men I've ever met, that says a lot for how much he must love your mom."

"Yeah." The silent tension had grown so thick over the years, she couldn't wait to leave for college. "Still, Chris and I weren't surprised when they drew up divorce papers. They had a tough start, followed by a rocky couple of decades before everything came together for them."

Saying it out loud resurrected memories of childhood nights crying in her bed while her parents fought downstairs. Crying harder when they stopped talking altogether. "So why did I wait? I just wanted to be really, really sure before I committed even a part of myself to a guy."

Would he freak out now? Or would she beat him to the punch?

Nerves pattered in her stomach as she realized how close she was to giving more than a part of herself to Carson, a man who didn't cry for himself, but teared up over Bronco's little girl possibly losing her daddy.

Jeez, how selfish of her to have forgotten what brought him to her in the first place tonight. "Are you okay after everything that happened this afternoon?"

"I'm leveled out now. Thank you for letting me spill my guts like that back in the truck." Before she could answer, he flicked the drain on the tub, water sucking out. "We should dry off before we turn into a couple of prunes."

Vulnerability might be long suppressed, but she'd seen his sensitive side now and couldn't forget. She hauled herself from the tub and grabbed a coral towel, reaching for another for Carson from the wicker basket, wishing they could simply dry each other off and go to sleep. Instead, she kept thinking about what demons must be rumbling around inside of him after a day like today. Leveled out wasn't the same as okay. She knew that well from watching her parents interact after her father's capture in the Middle East.

Carson's capture, as well.

Nikki tugged the towel into a knot between her breasts. "What happened today must have brought back some awful memories of your own time overseas."

He grunted, toweling his legs dry.

Carson never just grunted. He might dodge direct answers

but he was always, always polite. She thought about backing off and letting him have his space…but then she remembered how that tactic had nearly destroyed her parents.

Holy cow, was she thinking about being a couple? Well, she wasn't *not* thinking about it. She couldn't lie to herself. She had feelings for this man that deserved exploring, which meant no half-measure crushes where they never looked below the surface.

Towel drying her hair, she stared at his steamy reflection as he stood behind her tying his towel around his lean hips. "I heard my dad's version of what happened to your crew overseas." The towel slid from her shaking hands. Kneeling, she scooped it into the hamper. "It took him a while to talk about it, but after he and Mom started marriage counseling, they decided Chris and I should know what happened when he was shot down and captured by those warlords. We're adults after all. They both decided they'd sheltered us too much from things growing up."

"Do you agree?" He draped his dog tags around his neck.

Tugging the comb through her gnarled hair, Nikki wished her life could be as easily untangled. "Certainly Chris and I knew something was going on between Mom and Dad. It was tough growing up with him gone so much, and Mom pretending everything was fine."

She turned to lean against the vanity, taking in his golden gorgeous face marred only by a tiny scar along his jaw. A scar that somehow made him all the more handsome for the human imperfection.

A scar he'd gotten during his time in the Middle East.

She traced the faded white line cutting through his five o'clock shadow and wondered about the scars he carried inside from his childhood, as well. "Hearing the truth might have reassured us since sometimes reality isn't as bad as what you're fearing."

He enfolded her hand and pressed a kiss to her wrist, right on her racing pulse. "You're talking about something else now."

"And you're a perceptive man."

Carson dropped her hand and strode from the bathroom. "If you're thinking about my parents, the reality is at least as harsh as whatever you would imagine."

The tile chilled under her feet as she stood in the doorway. "They hurt you?"

His back to her, he snagged his flight suit off the rocking chair in the corner. "Coked-up people don't know their own strength and lose a lot of inhibitions."

She wanted to wrap her arms around his waist, press her cheek to his shoulder, but she also didn't want to risk stopping his flow of words. She sank to rest at the foot of her bed in the middle of tangled sheets and the scent of them together. His handkerchief rested folded on top of her laundry and she still didn't know what that middle initial stood for.

Had anyone ever cared enough for this man to know everything—even the darker things—about him? "I'm so sorry."

"Don't get me wrong. I could handle getting slapped around, and I could defend myself when one of Mom's stoned friends came barging through my bedroom door."

A gasp slipped free. Her fears hadn't even come close to the reality.

He glanced over his shoulder, face harder than she could ever remember seeing it. "I was fine, Nikki, but when I caught some high bastard on top of my sister…" Turning away again, he yanked the uniform zipper up his body. "I went to one of my teachers for help. Other teachers and even the cops had blown us off in the past—or my folks bought them off. Who knows? But this teacher, Mrs. Godeck, she was different. Stronger. She told my parents she was going to make their lives hell if they didn't send us both to boarding school. Somehow, she stood them down."

Thank God for Mrs. Godeck.

He dropped into the rocker and laced his black combat boots, left, right, done. "Are you ready to go back to your folks' place? I need to report in early today and take care of all the fallout from the barracks bombing."

She was sitting in her towel, for heaven's sake, and it was—she glanced at the clock—four in the morning. Unease prickled. He couldn't be walking on her again because she'd gotten too close….

"I'm not walking out," he echoed her thoughts so perfectly it spooked her. "I truly do head into work at five or six on a normal day."

"And this isn't a normal day."

Taking her hands, he knelt in front of her. "Not by a long shot."

His explanation made sense, but still, something wasn't right. "I understand about commitment to your job."

He squeezed her hands. "I want you to be careful when you go back to work."

"Of course I will."

He could take his distance and shove it. She kissed the faded scar. "I'm also checking in this week with Reis about some thoughts I've had."

And to find out more about those creepy calls to her parents' house. She wanted more facts before she told Carson so he wouldn't freak needlessly and lock her whole family in some hotel until her father returned.

Carson tapped her forehead. "Memories?"

"Ideas."

"Good ones?"

"Crummy ones, actually, but I hate feeling helpless."

His throat moved with a long swallow. "Helpless sucks."

For a second the connection between them shimmered to life again, a thin, fragile thread she needed to handle with a feather-light touch.

From his thigh pocket, his cell phone chimed—at four in the morning? The thread snapped.

He growled. "I'm starting to hate that damn thing." Rising, he dropped a quick kiss on her lips as he whipped his cell phone from his pocket. He glanced at the LCD, his face blanking. "Sorry. I have to take this."

Carson stepped out onto the balcony to talk in private, his voice low. Even with his reassuring kiss and words, she couldn't shake the feeling there was something more he was keeping from her. She thought about those two men she'd seen him with the night of Gary's death, and how Carson had neatly avoided saying anything about them when she shared the memory.

Staring at the broad plank of his shoulders as he stood outside taking his mystery call, she told herself they were still early in this relationship thing. Be patient. Build trust.

Except she couldn't help but think of how long her mother had told herself the very same thing.

Chapter 11

Sliding the balcony door closed behind him as he stood outside in the chilly night, Carson tucked the phone to his ear, his head still pounding from the discussion with Nikki. He was trying, but he couldn't miss the searching in her eyes, the need for something more he wasn't sure he had in him to give after his screwed-up childhood.

However at the moment, the person on the other end of the phone needed him. That loyalty had to be a top priority. Without the support system, none of them would be worth a damn to anyone. "Hello?"

"Carson? Will, here. Sorry to call so late." They used first names in the program, even when they knew the surname.

"How's everything going?" All right, he hoped, because as much as he tried to channel his thoughts into being supportive, he couldn't stop thinking about Nikki, being with her—and the mind-blowing discovery that they hadn't been together months ago before he'd passed out.

He'd always been a heavy social drinker. That sense of family in a gathering had sucked him right in and he would stay until the bell rang for last round. He'd tried a few times to cut back, but with no lasting luck—until he'd bottomed out that night with Nikki and realized he needed to join A.A. He still had a long road ahead, but his sea legs were back under him and he owed a debt for that.

Free time was in short supply, but he volunteered every spare second to a local support group that served as a catchall for relatives of people with a variety of addictions. "Hey, Will? You still there?"

"Yeah," the older man cleared his throat, voice raspy from years of smoking to fill the empty hours without a beer at the racetrack, "Vic called."

Not Will's problem tonight, but rather the guy Will was sponsoring. Will had been sponsoring Owens, as well, since Will belonged to both AA and Gambler's Anonymous. "At four in the morning? Must be bad, but at least he called."

Vic Jansen had caught the potential drinking problem early, recognizing he was having a rough time since he'd lost his daughter, using alcohol to numb the pain. Carson had a feeling Vic would make it through, and once he had his life back, the guy had the makings of being a rock-solid support. But first, they had to get Vic to tomorrow.

"He needs someone to come over and talk. My boy wrecked the truck and I don't get it back until the morning…"

"I can cover it." Easy enough to drop in since Vic lived on

his forty-two-foot sailboat docked near Carson's smaller one. Hell, he understood well how tough the nights could be. At least Vic was making the call rather than landing on the wrong woman's doorstep. "Thanks for the heads-up."

"No problem. Let me know how it goes."

"Roger." Carson disconnected and stuffed the cell phone back into his flight suit pocket.

Now he needed to figure out how to leave without seeming to bolt through the door. He wasn't sure where he and Nikki were headed, but again she'd held him through a hellish night. As much as he didn't want to lean on anyone, he couldn't ignore the fact that he kept ending up on her doorstep when *he* needed someone.

Which cycled him back around to being a taker, the thing he hated most. So what the hell to do? Deal with it one day at a time until he got his head out of his butt.

He rolled the glass door open to find Nikki dressed again. God, she looked great in those short fuzzy sweaters, softness and bright colors calling to his hands, *touch me*. He cricked his neck through the temptation to explore tangerine angora. "I'm sorry. I have to go."

"Work." Kneeling, she nodded, fishing a canvas bag from her closet, the hem of her sweater inching up to reveal a strip of her creamy back. "I understand."

Work? Carson hesitated a second too long and she glanced over her shoulder. He wasn't fooling her for a second, but couldn't say more. "I would stay if I could."

He hated lying to her. For the first time he considered telling her about his alcoholism. Why had he held off so long? Had he been enough of an ass back then to keep the secret so as not to taint her hero worship? A distinct possibility he needed to make right, and soon.

At least then she would understand moments he had to leave at the drop of a hat for a non-work-related call when he couldn't give her the specifics. That confidentiality was crucial in A.A., something he couldn't break even for Nikki. It sucked bad enough that Reis had investigated Owens's sponsor. How he'd found out the confidential relationship, Carson didn't know.

Okay, so he would tell Nikki about his drinking problem, but it wasn't something he could drop on her then sprint out the door. And he *did* have to sprint. "We're still on for sailing this weekend?"

"Sure." Canvas bag at her feet, she tugged open a drawer and shuffled clothes into the sack.

Thank goodness she was packing. While he was okay with them hanging out here together for a few hours, having her move back in—alone—was another matter altogether. Hopefully this hell would be over before she needed to use all those socks.

And satin underwear. Mint-green. Grape-purple. Lemon-yellow and funny how the mind focused on food adjectives for tasting. Tasting her. Was she wearing tangerine-orange to match that sweater?

Think of something else, pal. Pronto.

His fingers grazed a notepad by her phone, tore off a piece of paper and started folding. He'd picked up origami on his own one dark night, desperate to keep his hands busy with anything other than a bottle.

"I'll call." And he would. She was just within her rights to doubt him. *Fold. Tuck. Don't touch Nikki.* "Come on and I'll drive you back to your parents' place—and don't even suggest staying here."

"I'm not reckless. I know that I'm not some supercop or investigator. I'm a teacher, something I hope I'll be allowed to do now that I'm off the official suspect list."

She slid a neatly pressed pair of khaki pants from the drawer and he realized she was packing work clothes. Of course she would return to her job now that her name was cleared. Back to students who slashed tires and schools with metal detectors.

He forced himself to breathe evenly and crease the edge of the tiny form taking shape. "Do you have a gun?"

"No." She dropped another sweater, purple to match that grape lingerie no doubt. "And I'm not going to keep one with Jamie around."

"Fair enough."

He knelt beside her, his hand falling on top of hers to stop her speedy stowing because too easily he could envision her someday packing up to walk out of his life for good. "I really am going to call."

"Of course you are." Her hair swished forward to hide her face. "Carson? What's your middle name?"

Huh? God, he would never understand women.

He cupped her head, silken strands sliding over his skin until finally she looked up at him. "Alexander. My full name is Carson Alexander Hunt the fourth."

Searching her translucent gray eyes, he found wary consent a second before her hand glided up to his shoulders. Her mouth met his, no doubt about the mutual move. Here at least there were no misunderstandings or hesitations, just a driving need.

And if he didn't stop soon they would be doing a lot more than kissing.

He eased back. "I don't want to rush all the things I have to say, but come this weekend, we need to talk."

Her fingers toyed with the nape of his neck, her lips teasing over his. "I'd rather do more of this."

He pressed the one-inch paper tulip in her palm. "Certainly possible."

If she didn't run screaming and packing for good after their conversation.

Her every nerve screamed with tension.

After a jam-packed week of waiting to be alone with Carson, Nikki batted three helium balloons down and out from the passenger seat of her Ranger, clamping a folded Welcome Home, Dad banner under her arm. The three Mylar balloons would be a flyaway mess on the flight line, but Jamie loved them so she'd decided they could just tie the red, white and blue trio to her little brother's wrist.

Patriotic balloons trailing after her, she made tracks toward the big blue Air Force bus that would transport the families out to the tarmac to greet the returning aircrews.

True to his word, Carson had called her, every day this week for that matter, always checking in with her brother, as well, for a security update. Carson had even sent her flowers the morning after they'd made love. Not generic red roses, but a dozen, each one a different color. The note read how they reminded him of her sweaters and the brightness she brought to his life.

She'd cried—who wouldn't?—and slipped the card into the plastic picture holder in her wallet along with the origami tulip so she could look at both again and again in hopes of overriding the impending sense of doom. Their quick conversations had done little to diffuse the anxiety. His workweek was insane with the bombing and returning flyers. And since her return to the classroom, she'd been playing catch-up.

They were talking, some of the conversation sexy and longing. He wanted her. No question. It wasn't like before. But still... She'd been hurt, then angry for so long, this shift left her a bit off balance.

Panting puffs in the cold, she made it to the bus and climbed up the steps with seconds to spare. She waved to her mom and brothers in back and plopped in the lone remaining seat up front. Surely she would feel better once her father was safely home, then she and Carson could have their sailing date.

Date.

For real this time. Her hands clenched around her purse with that silly-sweet note from Carson inside.

Brown and brick buildings sprawled on the other side of the windows, reminding her when somehow she'd ended up here in a VOQ room with Gary Owens. God, she'd done a one-eighty from before, being certain the time had come to leave Carson Hunt behind forever. Now that she wasn't so focused on jabbing pins in a Carson voodoo doll, she was reminded of all the things she'd liked about him the first go-round.

He had a way of finding a good quality in each person and relating to them on that level, rather than seeing the negative and judging. He excelled as a leader by giving everyone else a chance to succeed based on that strength, something she would do well to cultivate in her teaching.

The lumbering bus jerked to a halt on the tarmac, restless families standing, pouring down the steps. Rows of parked cargo planes loomed, waiting for their missing friends. Airmen lined up outside to escort the families and greet their returning squadron mates. Where was Carson? Somewhere in that crowd most certainly, since already in the distance, she could see the specks of approaching C-17s on the horizon.

Coming home.

Hugging her coat around her, she waited alongside the idling bus while people streamed out, her mom and brothers at the back of the line.

Kevin Avery peeled away from the other flyers in leather jackets and joined her. "Hey, Nikki. How's it going?"

She felt bad about the way she'd treated him back in "Anybody-But-Carson" dating days. He seemed like a nice guy, dedicated to his Air Force career. Thank goodness he was okay with being friends, and had even set her up with his buddy Gary.

Great. They all knew how that one had ended. "Everything's better. My dad's coming home and he's in one piece."

"Yeah, and I hear the investigators cleared you." He nodded, clean-cut hair, boots perfectly polished until they glinted in the afternoon sun. "That's good. I always knew it couldn't be you and I told Agent Reis the same."

Nikki scratched the back of her neck, but the itchy sensation persisted that she was being stared at. She turned, scanned the cement expanse. Carson was watching.

Watching her with Avery.

Darn it. Was Carson going to get all weird again and insist he was too old for her? She winced to think of herself two years ago *hoping* he would be jealous and notice her. How juvenile it sounded now. She truly had been too young for him then—what a surprise notion.

She wanted to reassure Carson that her eyes were so full of him that even when he wasn't around, no other guy existed. But he was working and she knew from years listening to her parents that PDAs—public displays of affection—while in uniform were frowned upon.

But a smile would be cool. Right? Just as she started to grin at him—

Carson winked. Quick. Then done. But the tingle lingered long after he turned away to speak with the aviators lining up in front of him.

And my goodness, she could sure keep staring at the tempting view of his oh-so-perfect tush in a flight suit, but someone might notice and she wasn't ready to go public with their relationship. Not yet.

If nothing else, she should let her parents know, although her mother had probably already guessed.

Her gaze skipped down and away, back to the present where… Oops. Kevin Avery had picked up on every bit of the exchange. She saw things through his eyes and her quick shuffle from Gary to Carson didn't look good. As Gary's friend, Kevin had reason to be confused, even pissed on his buddy's behalf. He had no way of knowing that she and Gary had already been finished. Even if she explained it, who's to say he would believe her?

She simply stared at him silently, fairly certain he wouldn't confront her if she didn't broach the subject.

He tipped his head toward the cluster of flight suit-clad aviators. "Guess I should line up with the rest of the welcoming committee. Glad you're doing okay."

As Kevin melded in with his friends, her mother sagged to sit on the bottom bleacher, the middle trimester of pregnancy already slowing her down while Chris followed with toddler Jamie.

Nikki extended a hand. "Hey Chris, let me see the little guy."

Rena grinned, taking the banner. "So Chris can catch me if I topple over the side."

"You said it, Mom, not me."

Squatting in front of Jamie, Nikki tied the ribbons around his chubby wrist, her heart squeezing as tight as the knot over how darn cute her youngest brother was. She hitched him up onto her hip and snuggled him close while pointing out airplanes.

Which took her eyes right back to the flyboys. Carson's eyes held hers across the tarmac. No wink needed this time. She saw it in his eyes, a warming. He definitely wanted her. She shivered.

"Are you cold, sweetie?" her mother asked.

Totally scorching inside. And oooh, wasn't that a tingly thought? Scorch inside her. "I'm fine, Mom, thanks. Just remembering how many times we've done this welcome-home gig."

And wasn't that a nontingly thought?

Then Carson's gaze slid to Jamie and her heart squeezed tighter, more so when something bleak sent clouds chasing through Carson's beautiful blue eyes. What could he want to talk about when they went sailing? They couldn't be jumping to a superserious level this quickly, and frankly, she wasn't sure she trusted him that much yet.

Shoot, she wasn't sure she trusted *herself* that much. None of which she needed to think about now anyway.

The cargo planes slowed to a stop, side stairs and back hatches lowering until each clanked on the ground. The high noon sun reflected off the lumbering beasts. People packed the bleachers and milled around at the side, excited chatter the common denominator.

How many of these had she waited through, waiting for her dad, holding her mom's hand tight like now? How many more might she wait through for Carson? He stood to the side with the rest of the squadron at attention as the cargo hold full of green-suited bodies came into view.

First down the ramp, a stretcher carrying Bronco. He'd made it through surgery, surprising everyone with his sturdy constitution by being cleared for transport to come home with his squadron. Never leave your wingman.

He would spend a couple more weeks in the hospital here, but with his doctor wife to keep him on his toes, he would be fine. Joker strode beside him with his arm in a sling, his free arm extended for his fiancée.

Yet even with the smiles there remained an underlying solemnity for the missing man. Gabby's body had already been flown to the small Maine town where he and his wife had been

high school sweethearts. The base had held a memorial cere-
mony that left her hands trembling, even now just remembering.

And then from the middle of the mayhem emerged her
burly father, big and alive, someone she'd alternately adored
and resented all her life, depending on which country he
parked himself in at the end of the day.

She liked to think she was past those childhood hang-ups,
but couldn't ignore how messed up her life had become lately.
She hated to think that her crush on Carson had been some
sad father-figure deal. Ugh. Regardless, she knew her feelings for Carson were anything but familial.

Her father pulled back from Rena and turned to his two
adult children, little Jamie scooped up in one arm.

"Hey, Daddy." Nikki stepped into his open arm. "Welcome
home."

"Thanks, baby girl." He dropped a kiss on top of her head,
a quiet stalwart man who somehow still left such a void of silence when he was away.

She blinked back tears she refused to let mar this homecoming and stepped aside. Rena returned to J.T.'s side, so
much love humming between them, Nikki inched farther
away to give them more space even in public.

Her mind winged back to her father's return nearly two
years ago after being shot down and captured, how her heart
had been in her throat waiting for Carson, too. By letting Carson into her bed, yes, she was entertaining ideas of forever.
She couldn't ignore it. Some folks had a more casual approach to sex, and that was fine by her, but for her life, she
simply wasn't wired that way.

She was well-equipped for military life, she understood it, she'd lived it. She knew all the jargon, headaches, *heart*-aches—the joys, as well. Yes, she could handle this with her hands tied behind her back.

But did she *want* to spend the rest of her life waiting on a tarmac with tears in her eyes?

Carson hated waiting. And waiting to get Nikki alone this week had been hell.

Only a couple more hours until duty could be placed on the back burner for the night. First, he had to finish in-processing the returning squadron members—paperwork, customs, turn in medical records and equipment while the families passed time at an informal gathering inside the squadron briefing room.

Not much longer and things would wind down. He strode through the corridor from his office back toward the buzz of voices. A door swung wide from the public bathroom. He dodged, just as Nikki stepped out.

Thank you. A reward at the end of a killer week.

He stepped closer without touching. "Hey you."

She smiled back. "Hey *you*."

"I've been going crazy this week wanting to see you." He advanced again.

Nikki stayed put, her smile full but her eyes…sad? "I understand you're busy."

Did she want space? Jesus, he was thirty-five years old, way past college-type dating scenes. Honesty. If they didn't go with that, then they were screwed.

He cupped her elbow and ducked into his office, door still

open but out of the mainstream of nosy folks. Clear for the moment, he allowed himself to move closer, near enough to exchange body heat as he flattened his hand on the wall behind her. "Just because I'm busy doesn't mean I'm not thinking about you."

Her smile filled her eyes now, too, breezily confident Nikki meeting him one for one. On a sexual level they were able to communicate openly. "And what did you think about when I crossed your mind?"

While they were being honest… "You usually crossed my mind naked."

"Totally?"

"Would it be piggish of me if you were only wearing heels?"

"Do-me pumps? Hmm… I may own a pair."

"Really?" He couldn't disguise his surprise. She'd never been much for heels, but then her barefoot appeal turned him inside out more than any other woman in stilettos ever could.

"No, I don't." Her grin went downright wicked. "But I will by this weekend."

He let his growl of appreciation rumble up and out as finally he got to be near her again. "How much longer until we can be alone?"

"What color?"

"Color?"

"Heels." Just below his neck, she toyed with the tab on his uniform zipper. "Since I'm shopping you can put in your order. Red or black? What's your pleasure?"

"You." He canted closer, a whisper away from her lips glistening with a gloss he would have to kiss off soon. He ducked his head close to her ear to whisper, "And I very much want to be your pleasure once we're out on the ocean, away from the rest of the world, no heels, no clothes, no outside worries. I wish it was summer so I could love you on the deck, out in the open, kissing every inch of your body while the sun does the same."

Her hot, panting breaths puffed over him. "Close the door. Now. Five minutes. Nobody'll miss us."

His brain fogged with possibilities of what they could accomplish in five minutes.

"Scorch?" a bass voice echoed down the hall.

He hadn't even heard anyone approaching. Jesus, he was far gone. Carson jerked, kicking himself for being reckless with Nikki's reputation and glancing back over his shoulder to look at…

The father of the woman he was just propositioning.

Gulp. Carson braced. "Yes, sir?"

J.T. frowned, stayed silent.

Sir. Crap. Carson's hand fisted on the door. He, a major, had just called a chief master sergeant *sir.* Officers did not call enlisted troops *sir.*

But a man sure as hell said *sir* to the father of his girlfriend. So much for waiting for the perfect time to logically explain about his relationship with Nikki.

They were so…

So…

Busted.

Chapter 12

She was so busted.

Three hours later tucking her little brother into bed, Nikki knew the confrontation was coming, even if her father had pretended nothing was wrong at the time. A quick unspoken agreement had zipped between the two men as readable as any newspaper.

No scenes at the squadron. Not a surprise since she'd lived her life being told to wear her best face on base. Be a good reflection of her father. She knew the drill.

Carson had backed away, his sexy proposition still echoing in her mind and pulsing heat through her veins. They'd returned to the gathering as if nothing happened—except that her dad had stuck to her side like glue until they drove home.

She tucked the Bob the Builder sheets around her little brother in his new race car toddler bed. He already snoozed away on his stomach, diapered butt up in the air under the quilted spread.

She glanced over her shoulder at her mom in a rocker with her swollen feet propped on the edge of the mattress. Nikki settled on the remaining patch of bed, next to her mother's puffy toes. "Are you sure you don't want me to keep him up at the apartment so you and Dad can have the run of the house?"

Rena patted her rounded stomach. "I'm not so sure we'll be doing any running, but we may take you up on the baby-sitting service for an afternoon sometime soon. For tonight, I think Jamie needs routine and to be near his daddy."

She totally understood and agreed. "People say kids are flexible, but I see in the classroom all the time how they thrive on structure."

"There's so much about the military way of life that's not normal for kids, I've always tried to keep what I could constant."

"I turned out okay for the most part." Other than a dead ex-boyfriend.

"I hope so." Rena nudged Nikki's hip with her crossed feet. "We're certainly proud of you."

"Thanks. I'm trying my best, even if I screw up."

All that water retention in her mother's toes tugged at Nikki's heart as she thought of the grief she'd brought during an already stressful time. She may not have actually wielded whatever bashed in Gary's skull, but she'd been on a self-destructive path for months.

Could she trust her judgment to have magically improved now? "I'm sorry I've caused you and Dad so much heartache the past few months."

Her mother studied her through perceptive eyes, taking a slow swallow from her glass of ice water while a couple of trucks growled along the deserted night road outside. "Do you want to tell me what happened to send you into such a tailspin last spring?"

"Not really. Sorry." Telling would only make her mother upset with Carson when their relationship was about to become public. Really public, if the frozen tension on her father's face was anything to go by.

She should say something to her father before bed, even though she and Carson had discussed speaking with her father in the morning. Her mother wouldn't be surprised. She must suspect from how much time Carson had been spending around the house.

Had she known before? That "Mom Radar" was a spooky, perceptive thing.

Nikki refused to fidget like a kid. She was an adult. She didn't need her parents' permission, but she didn't want to make things tough at work for Carson or her dad. "I should let you go so you and Dad can enjoy your reunion."

Rena showed no signs of budging from her comfy spot. "I can talk a little while longer. Your father's busy for the moment anyway."

"Busy?" Uh-oh. Premonition trickled down her spine like the beads of condensation on her mother's glass.

"He's out on the porch waiting to talk to Scorch."

"*Sir,* huh."

The sardonic words from an obviously pissed off papa echoed across the lawn as Carson opened his truck door in the Price driveway. Looming on the porch, J.T. pinned him with a shotgun-father look as piercing as any bullet, illuminated all too clearly by the lamppost.

Carson finished stepping from his truck, not at all surprised to find J.T. waiting for him. They'd both known he would come by, an unspoken agreement.

At least the irate father hadn't made a scene at the squadron in front of everyone, because Carson damn well wouldn't have stood for Nikki's name being tossed around. As if she hadn't already been through enough gossip lately.

Thank God, her father apparently felt the same.

But now, after all the welcome-home partying was done, there was no more evading the question that had dogged the man's eyes throughout the evening.

"About that 'sir' thing…" Carson climbed the front steps, meeting J.T. face-to-face. "You caught me unaware. My nanny ingrained in me young to respect my elders."

"Elders?" Biceps flexed inside his flight suit. "You're really not getting on my good side today…*sir.* And I'm thinking it's important to you to be on my good side."

No-damn-kidding. Nikki was tight with her family, one of the many things he respected about her, and he refused to cause friction in the Price household. "I don't want to cause your daughter any grief and if you're upset that would upset *her* very much."

A vein pulsed in J.T.'s temple, a bad sign from such a usually laid-back guy. "Is there something going on with you and my baby girl?"

Baby girl?

Carson exhaled a long stream of cloudy air. He was definitely too old for this. But then he was dating a much younger woman, and hell, he wished his own parents had given a crap about his sister. He searched for the right words, the whole tongue-tied feeling completely alien for him, but then choosing the right words had never felt so important.

J.T. stepped closer, nose to nose and apparently more than a little miffed at Carson's extended silence. "*Sir,* I'm finding it hard to remember you're an officer. I'm finding it even tougher not to kick your ass off my porch."

"Go ahead. I was the one who peeled away the rank in there when I called you *sir.*"

"It's one thing if you're seriously dating, but if you're using her—"

Anger snapped. "Hold it right there." He didn't get outright mad often, but then nothing was logical in his head when it came to Nikki. "I respect your daughter and count myself one lucky bastard that she chooses to be with me."

J.T. pivoted on his boot heels away, chewing on a curse worthy of the saltiest of crewdogs.

Well damn. That was a little insulting.

A lot insulting.

He understood about the older man's wish for a nonmilitary life for his kids, but hell, he wasn't a total slouch.

J.T. cricked his neck from side to side before turning back around. "Is this serious? And don't tell me to ask her. I'm speaking with you."

Carson stepped alongside the old loadmaster and leaned his elbows on the porch railing while a rusted-out truck chugged past, exhaust mingling with the scent of mulchy leaves. He scrounged around for the right words to make this better for Nikki, for this man he'd flown combat with, a lasting bond. "I've heard you say for years no flyboys for your little girl. Was that bull?"

"I want an easier life for her than this—" he gestured back and forth to their uniforms "—a husband who's always gone, and getting shot at too often."

Husband. He didn't even bother denying the possibility existed. He tried a different tack. "You're speaking from a raw place right now because of the bombing and how close it hit."

"Could be." J.T. nodded a concession, ever fair. "Still, the military makes relationships tough enough, and I suspect you've got some extra stresses mixed in battling a drinking problem."

Ah. The real reason he disapproved. Somehow the seasoned chief master sergeant had figured it out when no one else had. "What makes you think that?"

"I don't talk much, but I'm always watching, and you go out of your way to avoid drinking, overly so."

"Plenty of people don't drink for any number of reasons."

"Are you telling me I'm wrong?"

When it came to Nikki, he needed to be honest every step of the way, because there wouldn't be another chance with her. J.T. wasn't the type to bandy the info around the squadron anyway. "You're not wrong. I wouldn't deny the problem if someone asked, but it's also not something I choose to advertise. I've been working at this for a couple of years, been completely dry and in a program for seven months."

Had he sealed his fate with Nikki's father? No hope for approval, ever? Entirely possible and totally more important than he'd expected.

J.T. sagged onto his elbows alongside Carson. "Thank you for being so open. I know that wasn't easy and it tells me you do care about my daughter."

Carson relaxed—for five whole seconds before he realized there was a *but* at the end of J.T.'s sentence. "And?"

"I respect like hell that you've fought this and seem to be holding your head above water. But you have to know this isn't something a father would wish for any child of his to live with."

"I agree." He had the same fears but staying away from Nikki had just about torn them apart. They needed to work through this insanity one way or another. "I've tried my damnedest to keep my distance."

"Tried." J.T.'s hands fisted before he continued, "Past tense?"

"Again, I'll say that I respect your daughter too much to discuss this further." The guy couldn't possibly want a blow-by-blow discussion. "Nikki's an adult. She deserves to be present so she can speak for herself."

"That earned you a couple more points."

Of course the conversation would have been a surprise for her if she had been here. "Nikki doesn't know about the drinking and I would appreciate it if you didn't say anything until I have a chance to tell her."

A slow growl echoed from the burly loadmaster's chest. "You've been seeing my daughter and you didn't tell her? I can't promise to keep quiet about that, and I'm actually reconsidering that ass kicking."

Well deserved. No denying. "I don't mean for you to stay quiet forever. Just until tomorrow to give me a chance to tell her first. We're going sailing."

"Twenty-four hours?" J.T.'s fists unfurled against his legs. "That, I can do, but the clock starts ticking now."

Wind rustled through the trees, shaking a few more pine needles loose in a *tap, tap, tap* shower that filled the semi-comfortable silence. "Still want to hit me?"

"Yeah." A hint of a smile twitched the corner of his mouth. "But I always want to hit anyone who looks at my daughter."

They shared a laugh and Carson started to hope that maybe…

J.T.'s smile faded altogether. "Hurt her, though, and I *will* make you hurt back."

Carson stifled a wince over the inescapable reality that J.T.'s warning had come a few months too late.

"Hope it's not too late for me to be here."

Her eyes full of hot and brooding Carson, Nikki stepped out to join him on the small landing connected to the garage apartment. "I couldn't sleep."

She'd given up at midnight, digging her way into a pint of ice cream to eat away the disappointment when he left without speaking to her after his conversation with her father. Five spoonfuls into her double-fudge chocolate, she'd moved from disappointed to peeved. How could he leave her hanging like that?

Except here he was before morning and her anger eased.

"How did things go with my father? I hope he didn't give you a hard time."

Her father had scooped her mom up and off to bed, their need to be alone so transparent she'd slipped away without speaking to him. He was due his reunion, but it pissed her off that her dad had still found time to speak with Carson.

Hello? Last time she'd checked, twenty-three was a legal adult age.

"Your dad was rightfully concerned and surprisingly understanding. I didn't get my ass kicked, so I guess it's all good."

"Sounds too easy, but I'm not going to complain." Nikki rubbed her bare arms in the running tank, her thin cotton sleep pants not providing much of a barrier against the chilly breeze. And also not the sexiest lingerie, complete with flip-flops instead of the fantasy heels.

"I'd planned to wait until tomorrow's sailing trip to talk to you, but I had to see you." His hand pressed to the white wood slats behind her, his body shielding out the world. "I've been dying to touch you all day."

She totally agreed, arching into his kiss, into this moment she so needed and deserved after a stressful week of waiting, wondering as she resumed her life. He cupped the small of her back, tunneled under her T-shirt, his hand branding all the hotter in forty-degree air. Her tingling toes curled, toasty warm even in flip-flops. The searching sweep of his tongue ignited sparks along her nerves until she itched to shed her clothes, tug off his…

Not a wise idea outside, especially at her parents' house with late-night traffic whispering in the distance, closer, the sound growing until a truck rumbled down her street, a vehicle apparently in need of a new muffler.

Carson's mouth stilled on hers, broke contact, a tension bunching muscles along his shoulders. She opened her eyes and found him scowling—but not at her, his attention focused on something over her shoulder.

"Carson?" She ducked her head into his line of sight. "Are you okay?"

He tucked her aside, while keeping his gaze on the road. "I've seen that battered old pickup drive past at least three times tonight."

She looked around his broad shoulders. "Do you think it's someone assigned by Agent Reis to watch the house?"

He urged her back toward the apartment. "I don't know, but it looks damned familiar."

"You're right." She held her ground, squinting in the darkness, and realizing— No. She didn't want that to be true, but couldn't ignore the obvious. "That's my student. The one you called a thug. Billy Wade Watkins."

Without a word, Carson lifted her by the waist, deposited her in the apartment and thundered down half the wooden steps before vaulting over the banister to the lawn. He sprinted across the grass and over a hedge, toward the street. Good God, he was going to get run over. Her brain went off stun long enough to race after him, double-timing the stairs to the yard, her feet in flip-flops slipping along the damp grass, slowing her dash.

Carson reached the truck as it finished a three-point turn. He yanked the door open and hauled the driver out by the sweatshirt. Most definitely Billy Wade Watkins.

Even under the mellow nimbus of the streetlight she recognized her student well, baggy clothes, body piercings and black do-rag tied around his head. Her heart broke a little more to think she could have misjudged him.

Wait, she reminded herself. Hear his story. And get over there fast before the vein throbbing in Carson's neck exploded.

Her feet quickly turning Popsicle cold, she danced across the yard. "Carson," she called out. "Everybody calm down." She sidestepped the walkway hedge. "Billy Wade, what are you doing over here this time of night?"

Carson's grip on the boy's hooded sweatshirt stayed tight. "And don't even try to say you were just driving around or some other BS answer. I've seen you case this house three times in the last couple of hours."

"Billy Wade? Did you really do that?"

His eyes actually filled with tears below his pierced eyebrow. "I was only looking out for you, Miss Price. I swear. You've been having so much trouble. You've been really good to me. I wouldn't do anything to hurt you."

She studied his expression, beyond the tears that could well be of the crocodile variety. He was left-handed, but strong enough to have swung with either. Yet he seemed to be telling the truth. Still she couldn't miss the additional glint of something more.

A crush.

Her heart hurt for the kid, but she couldn't ignore what logic told her, as well. This child was as big as an adult, and while she knew she hadn't done a thing to encourage him… And ah damn, what a time to be standing outside in her pj's, albeit more modest than most sleepwear.

"I think, uh, I'm afraid my dad might have been trying to hurt you." He swallowed hard, blinking back the glint in his big thug eyes. "Because maybe he's the one who killed that pilot and my old man's afraid you'll remember."

Nikki crossed her arms, rubbing away the increasing chill. "Your dad?"

"Yeah, he was that guy Owens's sponsor and they talked on the phone that day, and then Dad was out really late."

Carson's hand fell away. "You're William Watkins's son."

"Yes, sir. How do you know my dad?"

Carson hesitated, then answered, "Our paths have crossed at the base."

Carson didn't expand on the statement and just as she'd read the undertones in Billy Wade's eyes, she couldn't miss that Carson was hiding something now. Something she didn't have time to analyze as the porch lamp snapped on.

A door creaked behind her, broadcasting her awake household a second before her father burst onto the porch in sweatpants, tugging a T-shirt over his head. Her mother followed, slower, cinching her satin robe at her swelling waist.

Great. She'd wrecked her parents' reunion.

J.T.'s eyes radar-locked on Carson, then Nikki in her low-slung sleep pants and tight running tank, then right back to Carson again with a furrowed disapproval.

Geez, she was an adult woman. Her father really couldn't expect she would enter the convent. And darn, she had more important things to worry about now.

She was too old to be living at home, even temporarily. Yet as much as she wanted to politely tell her father to tone it down a notch, she couldn't ruin his homecoming. Besides, the cop sirens sounding from around the corner made a big enough to-do for one evening. Please God, this would clear away the chaos once and for all. And after the chaos?

Even with the end possibly in sight, she wondered if she would ever have the normal life she craved back again.

Chapter 13

A day out on the ocean felt too normal with Nikki along.

Although Carson figured they were both due some peace after the chaos of the night before. His eyes on the distant cove where he planned to anchor soon, he gripped the wheel, sunburst nylon sail stretching tauter, the hull slicing faster through Charleston Harbor on a cloud-free winter afternoon. Nikki stood in front of him, equally as tense in the bracket of his arms.

At least they were finally away from the prying eyes of her father—who'd stayed out in the dark yard working on bogus-ass tasks until Carson gave up getting Nikki alone again. Apparently daytime outings with Nikki were cool by the old guy.

Sailing had been his solitary escape, alone on the boat even when there were boats bobbing or skimming in the distance. While he'd thrown a couple of fishing parties in the past, he'd never used his boat for dates, something private that would invade his sanctuary.

Now whenever he stepped on board, he would always think of Nikki with her face tipped to the sun or her swishing ponytail pulled through the ball cap. Chocolate hair swayed in time with the boat's rhythmic cuts through the waves. Wind plastered her clothes to her lithe body he now knew intimately well.

And with that knowledge came a possessiveness he couldn't deny. He wouldn't be Neanderthal enough to voice it, but he couldn't ignore the primal pump of rage that still charged through him every time he thought about that teenage kid stalking Nikki. A kid who happened to be the son of Will Watkins, Gary Owens's sponsor.

The fact was now public knowledge, thanks to Billy Wade's outpouring to the cops. The kid swore his old man owed Owens gambling money. They must have fought that night and Nikki saw the accidental death that resulted. The boy had confessed to the hang-up calls, using pay phones to keep from being traced. He swore he'd been trying to get the nerve to tell Nikki his fears about his father, thus the hang-ups. He adamantly denied having anything to do with slashed tires and a loose railing. And the Rohypnol? That must have been from Owens.

Carson's fingers gripped the wheel tighter. This was all getting too weird for his peace of mind, but he'd had no reason to guess the kid at Nikki's school was the son of someone in A.A.

Reis was looking into Will Watkins's alibi that night. The military retiree had started out the evening with Vic and Carson, going to a meeting, but that had wrapped up by ten. What about after?

Will had some hefty demons on his back, battling drinking and a gambling addiction. Or had it really been the son, a jealous kid lusting after his teacher and trying to throw off the investigators in desperation?

At least Reis had solid leads to follow and Carson figured he would keep Nikki occupied and in his sights at all times. He just hoped what he had to tell her today wouldn't send her overboard.

Talking about his alcoholism never ranked high on his list of favorite pastimes, but he was getting better at vocalizing the feelings and experiences. Discussing it helped others just starting on the road to recovery. However telling Nikki and seeing the disillusionment in her eyes would be tough.

Autopilot activated, Carson stepped away from the wheel, untying lines to slow the boat and ready to anchor. Would she notice he'd brought them to the cove by the small battlefield landmark where they'd made love for the first time? The trees looked like any other, and the two lopsided cannons could have been from a dozen other sites. But he knew otherwise.

Damn. He was turning into a romantic sap. He welcomed the exertion to work off excess tension and the protective need to keep Nikki close. Safe.

Nikki caught his gaze with hers. "I'm okay," she said as if reading his thoughts. "Nothing happened to me last night."

He was in over his head with this woman.

Carson sidestepped away from her to drop anchor. "When I think of what *could* have happened to you, all those times you were alone with that kid…"

Restless, edgy, he tossed the anchor into the harbor with extra force.

"I was never alone with Billy Wade for just that reason." Nikki stowed lines, already having picked up on his routine with a perception and ease that further closed his throat.

Her words did little to erase hellish scenarios of other horrific possibilities. He was definitely in over his head.

Carson closed the gap between them and pulled her to his chest, not as gentle as he should have been but his emotions were far from temperate. "I just want to keep you safe."

"There's nowhere totally safe. Ever. For now could you stop thinking?" She stepped from his arms, holding his hand and backing toward the hatch that led to the cabin below. "Just feel."

He followed her step for step along the slick deck, grateful for the reprieve from discussion she unwittingly offered. He was only too glad to put off the inevitable. "There's nothing I want more than to feel every inch of you."

"Then by all means—" her hand releasing his, she shrugged out of her windbreaker and hooked her fingers on the hem of her pullover and tugged upward, right there out in the open air and cold "—indulge yourself to your heart's content."

Heart?

He suspected the word wasn't too far off the mark when it came to this woman. Her windbreaker and sweater fell around her feet, leaving her in her jeans and mint-green silky T-shirt.

His hands shook as he hauled her back into his arms, only a few feet away from the solitude belowdeck calling to him.

With an empty bed.

Tangled sheets.

And Nikki.

They would get naked very shortly, no question about it, but first he had to taste her, fully, without interruptions from stalker teens or inquisitive investigators. Wind gathered speed over the stretch of ocean, encircling their locked bodies until Nikki shivered in his arms. From cold or desire? Either way, reason to take this party downstairs.

Slanting his mouth over hers, deeper, hotter, he hadn't been this nervous about having sex with a woman since *he'd* been the virgin. Maybe that was the whole point. This wasn't just about having sex. He was making love to her, and as tenuous as their relationship was, this could well be the only chance he would have to pour everything into loving her.

"Thank you," she whispered against his lips.

"For what?"

"For bringing me here, to this place where we found each other for the first time. For knowing the gesture would be sweet and special."

And suddenly coming here didn't seem so sappy after all if it made her happy. Three steps down into the galley, then they stumbled backward toward the sleeping quarters. The bed stretched from side to side, no room to walk around, the mattress the only real place to sit—or lie—together out of the biting wind. *Yes.*

As if she'd heard his thoughts, she moaned her agreement into his mouth. Minimal light filtered through the rectangular portals, slanting illumination over the brown linens in their cavelike haven.

Her frantic hands tore at his jacket, then yanked his long-sleeved polo shirt past his head, sending it sailing to the floor at the same time he finally managed to peel up her neon T-shirt and, heaven help him, her matching green bra.

Damn, he loved her bright colors and the way they echoed the brightness inside her.

The boat rocked under his feet with the gentle slap of each wave against the hull, but the soft swell of Nikki's breasts above the lacy cups rocked him even more. A chilly gust of salty air blasted through the hatch, beading tempting breasts against satin, luring him to touch more of her. All of her.

His mouth exploring her neck, he reached behind to close the door. Darker. Warmer.

Alone.

Lowering her, he extended an arm to brace on the edge of the mattress until they stretched side by side along the brown comforter. Shoes thudded—*one, two, three, four*—onto the waterproof flooring. "Do you want—?"

"Yes. Totally. Want you to stop talking."

"Roger." He could think of better ways to occupy his mouth, especially since she seemed so intent on getting them both in the buff ASAP. He clicked on the miniature lamp mounted to the wall, intent on recording every inch of her to memory.

On her back, she scrunched down her jeans with an enticing wriggle and kicked them free, revealing matching mint panties and oh-so-long legs. His pulse spiked, couldn't possibly jump higher.

And then she proved him wrong.

Nikki skimmed her foot up over his ankle, rucking up his

jeans to burrow her toes higher, rubbing back and forth, skin to skin contact all the more intense as the stakes rose for them.

He released the front clasp on her bra, desire pounding harder, pulling tauter. He grazed hot kisses down her neck, lower, so slow, tormenting until she splayed her fingers through his hair and guided him to…

Yes.

He blew warm air over the heart of her a second before he tasted her essence—hot and moist. And apparently just what she wanted if her gasps and sweet whimpers were anything to gauge by, her legs widening to give him more. All. Her release came hard and fast, her clawing grip on his shoulders sending a bolt of pleasure throbbing through him. He held her thighs and soothed her through the aftershocks.

Confined in the cramped hull, she grappled with his jeans, unbuttoning the fly one strained pop at a time. Her hand slid inside and…

Uh, what was he thinking about?

His mind blanked, thoughts washed away along with all his blood flooding south. Jeans flew off as fast as what remained of his restraint. Fishing a condom from his wallet, he sheathed himself and rolled on top of her soft scented body, lowering himself, seating deep inside her.

Her legs locked around his waist, urging him to move, move again, endlessly with an urgency echoed inside him. The boat undulated with waves that left her clinging tight to him for anchor. The surprise surges heightened the pleasure, deeper, harder, then shallow and faster.

Until her toned legs demanded he give all. He gritted his

teeth through the blinding drive to finish. But not before her...not before...

Her scream sliced through his restraint like the hull of a boat parting a wave, the wake crashing into a churning tumult that lasted and lasted, finally fading. Shuddering in the aftermath, he sagged on top of her, her sighs heating over his neck. Her hands glided along his sweaty shoulders in featherlight touches that slowed along with her breaths at the onset of her nap.

Shifting to his side, he pulled her closer, holding her while she slept. No more delaying. He would have to tell her about his alcoholism, something that could, and very likely should, send her running.

Why hadn't he done this back when the prospect of losing her didn't rock him even more than facing combat?

Resting on her side, Nikki watched Carson's perfectly sculpted face as he slept, not a peaceful nap, but restless, mixed with the occasional twitch as if he might wake at any second. The tiny digital clock blared three in the afternoon, plenty of time to let him relax a while longer. She stretched her arm from under the fluffy weight of the comforter and clicked off the tiny light, casting the cavelike cabin and Carson's features in shadows.

She'd sensed a tension in him while they made love, connecting in some way that scared her to her toenails. She hadn't known the emotions would come so fast, so thick, swamping her in more—deeper—feelings for Carson than she'd ever dreamed. She wasn't so naive that she couldn't recognize the explosiveness of how he made her feel in bed.

Four orgasms in one afternoon was nothing to sneeze at, although he seemed to tease them from her as easily as an achoo.

She'd thought their first time making love had been special, even their abruptly ended encounter months ago. Now she knew none of it had come close to what had been waiting for them.

Because they knew each other better? Or cared more? Could things grow stronger?

The caring part scared her. Really scared her. Because she didn't trust him not to break her heart again if they got closer. Her cold toes warming between his legs, she allowed her hands the unobserved pleasure of touching him, stroking along his muscled arms that had held her close, down his chest and lower still to his six-pack, tanned even in winter.

She couldn't avoid hearing whatever he'd wanted to say much longer. She'd chased off admissions with sex earlier. But whatever he was holding back, his reasons for leaving her that had nothing to do with work, would all come out soon.

Along with his connection in knowing Billy Wade's father, a man with a gambling problem.

Nikki flipped to her other side, away for distance, her toes already chilling just seconds after leaving the warmth of Carson's legs. Déjà-vu jiggled the vision in front of her as she fell asleep, taking her back to that strange night.

Strange room.

Strange bed…

How had she gotten here in this strange hotel-like place? And who was talking, their masculine voices so low she could barely distinguish the two from each other as she sprawled on the bedspread?

She couldn't remember anything after she'd climbed into Gary's car, sleepy. So sleepy. Her head pounded. Her stomach roiled. A couple of drinks shouldn't have done this to her. What was wrong with her?

Voices. In the hall or in the room? She struggled to focus, but her heart in her ears pounded louder than the whispers. She peeled her eyes open. Gary and another man stood at the foot of the bed. So close, she should be able to hear them but the world kept kaleidoscoping in and out.

She studied the back of the second man. He seemed familiar, even in jeans and a leather jacket, his hair trimmed military short.

His blond hair.

Panic clenched a vise grip around her throat.

The man in jeans and an aviator jacket turned in slow motion. No! built in her chest, crawling up her throat to stop him and what she didn't want to see but already foresaw. The denial lodged in her throat and he kept pivoting until she saw...

Carson.

Carson cranked the anchor up, prepping the boat to set sail back to Charleston. Before they reached shore, Nikki would know every dark secret from his past. Although he almost wished now he'd broached the subject with her earlier, when she'd been in a more receptive mood.

Nikki had gone silent since he woke from his catnap, refusing to meet his eyes and he didn't have a clue why. Now she sat back by the wheel, studying the other boaters in the distance, hugging her knees as she stared out over the stretch of murky water. No ponytail or ball cap, just wild windswept hair and the elegant curve of her neck he'd explored with kisses a couple of hours ago.

Before she'd shifted to deep freeze mode.

Women were tough enough to understand on a regular day and never had understanding a woman been more important. Stepping over lines and a loose life preserver, he made his way toward her. She flinched. Flinched?

Once under full sail power, autopilot set, he asked the question burning his brain. "Is something wrong?"

She dropped her forehead to rest on her knees. "I'm just confused, that's all." She turned her face to stare back at him, tears in her eyes. "I want to trust you, but it's difficult when I can't help but think you're not being straight with me."

Had her father already spoken to her? Regardless, the time had come to tell her what he'd only discussed with J.T.—and a room full of people sworn to uphold the anonymity of the program. "I'm an alcoholic."

"What?" Her head jerked up, confusion chasing away tears. "Wait. I heard you, I just don't understand. You hardly ever drink. Even with your flaming Dr Pepper call sign, I can only think of one time I've seen you with alcohol."

One time, the night they'd been together.

But if she hadn't been questioning his drinking with her initial comment, what had she thought he was keeping from her? They would get back to that shortly.

"Yes, I was drunk the night we slept together." Guilt hammered all over again, as strong and fresh as the morning he'd dragged his hungover butt to A.A. "I'd been working on staying sober for two years until then."

A wry smile kicked through the furrows of confusion. "Great. I was a drunken mistake."

He was making this worse, and that was quite an accomplishment since the situation had pretty much sucked from the start. "You could never be a mistake. You are the most amazing, tempting woman I've ever met. The only mistake was my selfishness that night, because I knew I would hurt you eventually."

Her chin jutted with a quiet stubbornness he'd seen often in her father. "You hurt me by walking away."

And in that stubbornness he could see that, regardless of her words to the contrary, she hadn't forgiven him, not really. So why was she sleeping with him?

He'd assumed being her first meant he was somehow special to her. Now he wasn't sure of anything and he didn't like that feeling one damn bit. "I joined A.A. after our night together. I'd had blackouts before, but not one that led me to hurt someone. It was a wake-up call."

She blinked fast, straightening. "You had a blackout that night?"

"We discussed this before—the reason I didn't remember we never had sex that night."

"A blackout? You didn't remember anything?"

Hadn't he already said that? "Not much, no."

He wasn't sure if that helped her come to grips with this or not, but it certainly sent her eyebrows trenching deeper until she softened and leaned ever so slightly toward him. Her deep freeze seemed to have ended. He could all but see the wheels churning in her brain as she sifted through his words. A promising sign and incentive to keep spilling his guts even if the talk grated all the way up his throat.

Carson rested an elbow on the silver railing, the waves below offering none of their usual comfort or answers. He shifted his attention to the speedboat in the distance. "I've always known I wouldn't get married. That's the reason I dated women with zero interest in commitment, until you came along and I started questioning what I knew, damn it, what I still believe, but am having trouble holding strong all over again."

"Why are you so sure you shouldn't get married?"

"My parents were drug addicts. Two of my grandparents had substance abuse problems, as well as an aunt and a couple of uncles. I've stopped counting the cousins with chemical dependency issues." He ticked off the dreary stat count on his fingers. "It's in my genes and I've seen what it can do to a family."

"Did any of them acknowledge the problem or get help?"

"My dad tried, along with one of my uncles, a couple of my cousins. But even with all the successes in A.A., I've seen failures, too. Hell, I was a selfish failure with you seven months ago."

She shifted to face him, her hands falling to rest on his thighs and searing through his jeans. "So you're doing this totally selfless thing in pushing me away, which proves you're actually a really good man. You've put us in a no-win situation, pal."

He gripped her fingers. "Jesus, Nikki, you just don't know how bad it was."

"Or maybe I know how good it *can* be."

Her optimism could be contagious, dangerously so. "I'm glad that you've had a life that leads you to trust that easily."

"So you're walking out again?"

"We're on a boat. I'm not walking anywhere." They were definitely stuck here until they hashed this out one way or another.

Her jaw shot out again. "That's not what I meant and you know it."

"Being with you scares the crap out of me, no question about it. That night I saw you at Beachcombers, it rocked me. Hard."

The mast creaked and groaned as an ominous silence stretched between them. "And you've been dry since last May? No more blackouts?"

He'd already answered that once. What was she driving at? Even as he understood he hadn't done squat to deserve her trust, he couldn't escape the sense of impending doom, thickening the late-afternoon air. "I'll admit, seeing you at Beachcombers that night was tough for me."

The boat pitched to the side, mast cracking, leaning.

Falling.

Seconds away from crashing into Nikki.

Chapter 14

Screaming, Nikki grappled for the boat rail. Anything stable in her abruptly tilting world as the mast leaned, held only by a couple of pathetically frayed metal lines.

"Carson!" she shouted, extending her arm toward him as she slid backward, toward the ocean.

"Jump!" he barked back. "Get clear of the lines before the boat pitches—"

A crack split the air as the mast careened out of control. The boat lurched to the side, catapulting Nikki airborne with only a few frozen seconds to gather her thoughts before...

Water gushed up her nose. Frigid and dark as she sank, not at all like the clear depths of a pool.

Up or down? Nikki couldn't determine which way since the bubbles swirled all around. All she'd learned in swimming classes said follow the bubbles but the underwater world churned and her senses shrieked conflicting messages.

She kicked. Against seaweed? No. Stronger. Slicing. Lines from the boat.

Ohmigod. Panic urged her to gasp, but she kept her lips pinched shut. She struggled to slide the metal lines—shrouds, Carson had called them—off her ankle and wrist. *Shrouds?* How horribly ominous that sounded.

And what an interesting word to tell her little student later. What an off-the-wall thought that stung her eyes with tears over the possibility she might not get to share in expanding his vocabulary any longer.

The watery world closed around her, wrapping like a blanket. Or a sail. The fabric sealed to her skin.

Her lungs burned, her skin numbing. Her brain even more so.

Panic gave way to terror that this might really be beyond her control. She could die.

How could she have been caught so unaware that she didn't notice the mast crashing toward her until too late? She'd been obsessed with the dream of Carson in the VOQ room the night Gary died.

Carson. Terror squeezed tighter. Where was he? If he'd been knocked unconscious, he could be drowning even now.

No. Hell no. She wouldn't let it happen.

She didn't care what he may have done the night Gary died. If Carson had been there, she was certain he didn't remember…none of which mattered if she couldn't find him now. She kicked against the restraints seeking to suck her deeper, ignoring the bite of metal through her skin.

The bubbles sparkled, brighter, her head lighter, her arms

and legs sluggish even as she continued to fight. Not much time left. Now that she was seconds away from checking out, too, she realized that the image of Carson had come in a dream, not in a memory flash like the recollections she'd recorded in her journal. Her confused and terrified mind could well have been playing tricks on her.

Something bumped against her. The boat? A shark? She shivered even though she'd long gone beyond numb.

Light pierced her cocoon. Death? No. The sail parted, sliced open, Carson's form looming as he split the water with sluicing sweeps of his arms, a knife in his hand.

He was alive. Relief threatened to steal precious seconds. She had to help or he would die trying to save her.

Kicking, he plunged down, unwinding the line encircling her ankle while she loosened the snaking vise around her arm. *Freedom.*

He clamped her to his side, surging up. She blinked back unconsciousness, but couldn't escape the stab of guilt over even thinking he could have lied about the night Gary died. Carson may have kept the alcoholism a secret, but this man would never have let her hang for his crimes. That much, she knew with a certainty as strong as the muscled arm banded around her.

The world righted as her equilibrium returned, up, up, blasting through the surface by the wounded boat. The massive keel along the bottom had righted the craft, even if the mast stretched a good thirty feet or more along the water, lines and sails such a tangled mess she wondered how he'd found her, much less freed her.

His feet trod water, brushing her with vital reassurance. Still he held her. "Are you all right? The mast didn't hit you?"

"I'm fine." She gasped, lungs aching, her feet pumping now as well since she didn't have to worry about dragging him down. "Thank you. Ohmigod thank you. And are you okay?"

"Fine." He didn't look fine. In fact he looked really pissed, his eyes stormy below a purpling bruise on his head.

Well, she was petrified to her toes. Only an idiot wouldn't be. They were in near-freezing waters, and while there were boats in the distance, they needed to book-it over before somebody lost a foot—or worse—to exposure.

"Somebody's head's gonna roll for this." Anger simmering, Carson paced in a back office at Beachcombers, while Special Agent Reis jotted notes. "I'm thinking it's going to start with you soon, Reis, if you don't figure out who the hell's trying to kill Nikki before she remembers what happened."

The horror threatened to crash over him again as heavy as that boom. The mast giving way, tipping the boat, launching both of them into the water. Then watching Nikki sink in a tangle of shrouds and sail.

His boots pounded hardwood floors in the antebellum building, intense, louder.

"Major, I understand you're frustrated." The agent sat on the corner of a desk, working a piece of gum while he typed notes in his PDA. "A freezing dip in the ocean will ruin a good mood."

"No." He stopped short, the window behind Reis providing too clear a nighttime view of the dock where someone intent on harming them had lurked in the past couple of days. "A deliberately broken mast will do that to a person."

"We can't know that for certain until your boat has been recovered and examined."

Carson wrenched his attention off the dock, back to the present and getting answers this man had the power to provide. "And I'm telling you, I keep that craft in tip-top shape."

"You weren't at all distracted today?" The agent tucked his PDA into an inside jacket pocket. "Couldn't you have screwed up locking the mast in place?"

For a second Carson wondered if maybe...then as quickly shoved aside the doubts. "I've been sailing by myself since I was ten." Which now that he thought about it didn't sound all that safe, but he'd been an expert in ditching his parents and nanny in those days. "And on the job, my life and the lives of others depend on following checklists. I do not 'screw up' in the air or on the water. Inspect those lines. I bet you'll find someone filed through the metal just enough to weaken one or two of the shrouds. Even a couple of small cuts would be imperceptible to the eye, while posing an insidious danger. Once the sails filled and pulled the lines taut, it would continue to fray until it snapped."

"An angle to investigate. I'll look into that once your boat has been impounded. I'll also ask around about activity at the dock."

Tension downgraded to half power. The guy was doing everything he asked, keeping him posted with all the facts.

Or was he? Had they all been wrong to assume Reis was top-notch at his job?

The door swung open, Nikki stepping through in a borrowed jean jumper from the proprietor, Claire McDermott, the dress a couple of inches short on Nikki, but dry.

And tempting with that extra stretch of exposed leg.

Reis straightened from the desk, his interrogator-perceptive eyes ping-ponging between the two of them. "Ms. Price, I assume you're all right."

She pulled up alongside Carson, fidgety, but understandable given their ordeal. "I'm running out of those nine lives, but otherwise okay." Her gaze skipped around the room full of spice plants. "And, uh, I think I remembered something on the boat right before all of this happened."

What? Carson's attention snapped as taut as the lines right before they'd popped.

"It wasn't a full-out memory like the other times, more of a mishmash dream. But I'm certain of one thing." Her restlessness settled into steely resignation. "There was another person in the room with Gary and me that night. A man. A blond man."

The implication sucker punched him. No wonder she'd gone tense after their nap and then asked him about blackouts. She thought he'd gotten drunk, gone after Owens and then forgotten.

His alibi only lasted until two in the morning with the emergency on the flight line that had called him away from his meeting. So he had no way of accounting for the in-between hours—except for a freaking zoo of origami animals he'd folded through the night to distract himself from thinking about seeing Nikki at Beachcombers, knowing she was dating another guy.

Reis pulled out his Palm Pilot again. "That Watkins kid has dark hair."

Nikki winced. "Which he colors according to his mood."

"His father has gray." Reis clicked away while Carson's

mind churned through this latest revelation. "Could the man you're remembering have had silver hair instead of blond?"

"It's possible, but I don't think so. And the clothes didn't seem right for Billy Wade. Jeans and a flight jacket."

Which gave her all the more reason to doubt Carson.

Reis shoved off the corner of the desk. "That could still be the father since retirees keep their leather jackets. But are you sure it was a man? Women have short hair, too."

One of Owens's old girlfriends on a jealous rampage?

Reis's talent for thinking beyond an obvious assumption was promising—and frustrating. How the hell could they rule anyone out? A military man or woman, active duty or retired, blond or gray, who happened to be right-handed. That could be half the flying community.

Nikki closed her eyes as if trying to recapture the image on the back of her lids. "If it's a woman, then she's really tall. It's all fuzzy, but I'm almost certain it's a man." Her lashes fluttered open as she shook her head. "I'm sorry. That's all there is."

Screw keeping his distance. Carson looped an arm around her waist, so grateful to have her warm and alive against him, he didn't bother to hide his feelings for her. "I think that's enough for one day, Reis. The medics wanted to admit her, but acquiesced if she would promise to rest."

The OSI agent pocketed his PDA again. "I hear ya." Halfway to the door, he stopped. "She's still staying with her parents, right?"

"Hello?" Nikki stiffened. "*She* is right here—"

"Major," Reis continued, "how about once you take her home we meet back on base and go over some personnel files to see what we can dig up?"

With the horror of Nikki almost dying still pounding through his skull, there was nothing he wanted more than to keep her in his sight. But with her stiff in his arms and her avoiding his eyes, he couldn't help wondering if she needed space, and God knows he wanted to dig in with Reis and find something, anything, to nail the bastard who'd done this to Nikki's life.

Besides, after hearing the truth about him she might well decide to steer clear of him and he would have to love her enough to let her go.

Love?

Damn.

What a helluva time to figure that out.

Her feet would never be warm again. Nikki wasn't so sure about her heart, either.

Sitting at her parents' kitchen table, she shook the can of whipped cream and squirted a hefty swirl into the steaming cup of hot cocoa her dad had made. What a crazy—confusing—afternoon. Finally, Carson was being open and honest with her, or at least he had been until the boat nearly killed them. He'd switched into protective mode again, dropping her off at her parents' with a toe-curling but too-brief kiss, before meeting up with Reis.

In her soul, she longed to grasp this new chance with Carson, but her emotions were all so surface level and exposed. She had to get this right—for both of them. She wanted to trust what he said about having his drinking under control, but he'd tossed so many negatives about the situation her way. She needed to be responsible enough at least to think through them.

Her lumbering father dropped into the chair across from her, silently drinking from his mug. Even more quiet than usual as he studied her across the wooden expanse, a new piece of furniture she'd helped her dad varnish after he'd bought it at the bare-wood store.

For an overprotective parent, these past days couldn't have been easy for him. She passed him the can of whipped topping. "Are you okay, Dad?"

"I should be asking you that, baby girl." His gaze rested on the raw ring around her wrist where the sail lines had immobilized her underwater.

"And I'm betting that because I'm your daughter, today was tougher on your ticker than it was on mine." She cupped her hands around the warm porcelain.

"You might be right." He set his World's Best Dad mug down slowly, his hand shaking ever so slightly but oh so tellingly. "I owe Scorch for saving your life."

"Are you okay with me seeing Carson?"

He nodded, suddenly overly preoccupied with how the can of whipped cream operated. "I'm not sure it would matter to you if I wasn't."

She sifted that around in her mind while sipping, chocolate and cream flooding her senses with childhood memories of other shared cocoa and late-night chats with her dad. She loved her father, no question, but she wasn't his little girl anymore. "It wouldn't change my mind, but it would matter."

"I know about his history." He rolled the can back across the table to her, his rugged teddy-bear face so compassionate she wanted to crawl in his lap and cry as she'd done during elementary school days.

Was it so wrong to seek his advice? Was that a step backward when more than ever she needed to add years in wisdom to her adult résumé? Still she couldn't stop the words. "Am I delusional to believe I can handle a relationship with a recovering alcoholic?"

"You're too old for me to tell you what to do."

Was she? At the moment it seemed less mature to assume arrogantly that she had all the answers. "I'm learning that you're never too old to ask your father for advice."

"Which proves you really don't need me after all." He patted her hand clutching the whipped cream can in a death grip. "You're more than ready to leave the nest."

Parental approval sure did feel nice no matter what her age. She flipped her hand to link fingers with her dad. "Does that mean I'm out on the sidewalk?"

"Not hardly, baby girl." He squeezed back with a familiar comfort that stung her eyes with tears at this landmark moment.

She really was crossing into a new era of her life. Would it include Carson?

Nikki slid her hand away and took another warming gulp from her mug. "What made you and Mom stick it out so long even though things were rocky?"

"But we did quit."

"After over twenty years of working at it." She hadn't been surprised when her parents announced they'd seen a divorce attorney, but it still hurt even as an adult.

A rare smile creased her father's craggy face. "Your mother and I are particularly hardheaded. It took us a while to get it right."

"That doesn't help me much."

"I assume this isn't a rhetorical question."

"I wish. He also worries about me being too young. And I think he puts too much stock in *your* certainty that I'm not equipped for the stresses of being an Air Force wife."

"Whoa. Wait." He held up both palms. "Of course I don't want you to go through the struggles. This is a tough life after all, but I've never doubted for a minute that you can handle anything that comes your way as long as you go in with your eyes open."

"Who are you, and what have you done with my quietly looming overprotective father?"

His smile cranked broader. "Your mother and I are working on better communication. Never thought I would buy into the notion of counseling, but it helps. What your mother and I have is worth fighting for."

She'd known they sought help to put their marriage back together. They'd even invited Chris and her along for a couple of family sessions. Why not apply that to her situation with Carson?

He assumed the alcoholism was more than she could handle. He might be correct—a possibility that closed her throat—but he might well be wrong. Either way, *he* had been making a decision that affected *both* of them. She should be a part of that equation, and to do that, she needed more information.

She'd been so set on protecting her heart, she'd let him shield her, as well, and that wasn't right. No one had ever fought for Carson. Sure he'd sought out A.A., but as far as she could tell, other than a lone English teacher, no one had offered help.

Yeah, she might get her heart pitched back in her face again, but she loved this man. Deep down loved him, flaws and all. Damn straight she wouldn't be like her mother waiting around for over twenty years.

Nikki was ready to fight for her man.

Chapter 15

"Do you want me?"

Carson lost total track of whatever Reis was saying to him on the other end of the phone, stunned instead by Nikki in his open office door.

From the determined look in her eyes, Carson suspected he had a fight on his hands. He just wished he knew which direction to check for the ambush.

He held up a hand indicating a one-second-wait while he finished his call to Reis about tapping the civilian police to do extra surveillance of the Price home. "Glad you're on top of this. I'll be in touch." He hung up the phone and redirected his attention to the hot-as-hell woman in front of him. "How did you get here? Please say you didn't drive alone."

"Dad's got leave since his return. He came in for some paperwork and I rode along." She lounged against the door frame, a seductress in khaki. "So? What's the answer to my question? Do you want me?"

"Before I answer, you should probably close the door."

Nikki stepped across the threshold, one long khaki-clad leg at a time—and holy crap, those were black heels to match her black silk shirt. Could her heels be the promised pair from their conversation a few days ago in this same room?

Tossing her lightweight jacket on the mariner's hook, she clicked the door closed and locked at the same time he instructed his secretary to hold his calls. Word was out about the two of them anyway, while he was still reeling from the whole concept of being in love for the first time.

They were already in over their heads, so he needed to grit back his concerns and forge ahead unless she said otherwise, because he wouldn't hurt her a second time.

He shoved aside the stack of files calling to him and wheeled his office chair back from the desk. "How about ask me that question again?"

Nikki narrowed the distance between them with hair-swishing strides. "Do you want me?"

That was a no-brainer. He took her wrist, careful of the raw ring from the lines, and pulled her into his lap. "So damn much."

Tunneling one hand into her hair and the other under her sweater, he kissed her until they both gasped for breath. He wouldn't be in any shape to get up from his chair for a long while, thanks to the sweet wriggle of her bottom against his crotch.

"Do you want to be with me? Not just tonight, but long term?"

He'd been prepared for her to walk, and now she was talking forever, something he couldn't deny that he wanted, too. With her. For a man with an extensive vocabulary, words were suddenly in short supply. He wouldn't run, but he couldn't blame her if *she* did.

"Damn it, Carson." She thumped his shoulder, then gentled her touch to skim tenderly over the bump on his head from pitching out of the Catalina. "Do you know how hard this is for me to say? I'm making myself totally vulnerable for you. The least you can do is give me an honest answer."

"Honestly?" There wasn't anything left for them but the truth. "I'm scared as hell of passing on my genes and I'm more afraid I'll ruin your life. You're not sure, either. Admit it, you thought I was the one who killed Owens."

That notion stung more than he would have expected even as she rested her head against his shoulder with total ease.

"If we're embracing this total honesty deal, then okay, I considered the possibility that you'd done it to protect me."

He struggled not to flinch. "You thought that, drunk, I would be capable of violence."

"I saw you in my dream." She tipped her head to glance up at him. Her silky dark hair grazed over his arm. "But I realize now it was a dream and not a memory, which means I've had to sift through to figure out which parts are real and which are distorted. The other times I remembered, I was awake so I could trust the full image."

"Are you sure?" He refused to have her fearing him. He'd lived that way for years as a kid and would *not* subject anyone to that hell.

"If you tell me, I will believe you."

Searching, he found trust in her eyes but couldn't bring himself to believe in what he saw. "So you do think I'm capable?"

"I know anyone is capable." Her fingers skimmed to the back of his neck, along his closely shaved nape. "I'm not sure I could kill someone coming at me. But I'm certain I could kill someone intent on hurting you."

He understood the feeling. "I did not kill Gary Owens. I was at an Al-Anon meeting that night with two other people," Will Watkins and Vic Jansen, "until I was called away to an emergency on the flight line. Then I went home and parked my sorry butt in front of the TV all night because I was missing you so much I was afraid if I went out I would end up on your doorstep."

Carson waited for her response, suddenly realizing that while he might not have a right to her unconditional trust, he sure as hell wanted it.

Finally, she nodded, rocked forward and pressed a long, close-mouthed but no less intense kiss to his mouth before settling to rest against his chest, arms still looped around his neck. "That's what I figured, but thank you for saying it for me anyway."

"Thank *you*." His arms slid around her and he stole a deeper kiss, needing to feel her warm alive body and banish the image of her wrapped in shrouds and a sail in a watery grave.

Her face tucked in his neck, she continued to tease his ear with feathery strokes that distracted. "Isn't Al-Anon a support group for family members?"

What had she just said and what did that have to do with

her other hand scratching through his flight suit along his pec? He replayed her words and—oh, uh, Al-Anon. Talk about a cold splash. "I help out there. The support group is open to helping families of people with other addictions. I feel like I have something to offer family members, as well, since my parents were addicts."

"So you belong to Al-Anon *and* A.A.?"

"Yes." Searching for words, he captured her hands in his, kissed her knuckles and kept them from distracting him into speaking without thinking, no doubt her intention. "Until I found A.A., nothing worked. It's still been tough. I truly believe that for alcoholics the booze affects them more or differently than other people. And through that extra effect it soothes something inside them, a pain or an emptiness or need. For a while you convince yourself the alcohol makes your life better. It's your friend because you live and cope at a higher level. Then the friend turns on you."

She linked her fingers with his so tightly he could imagine she might hold on forever.

"Those first few months without, there's this emptiness inside that begs to be filled. You also lose something in your way of life—the bar, the camaraderie of a beer and game of pool."

"I would imagine that's especially tough to give up in the flyer world."

"A.A. helps teach you how to fill that space, and of course there are over two million members."

"Two million?" Her eyes widened in surprise.

"And counting." He stroked the inside of her wrists with his thumbs. "I'm able to attend functions now that include alcohol without racing to phone my sponsor afterward— What are you thinking?"

She untangled her hand from his to tap his leather name tag. "How you said call signs come from a defining moment."

"I carry a heavy issue with me that's never going away." He rested his palm over hers tracing the word "Scorch." "This will always be there, and I know too well that it doesn't just affect the adults. While I appreciate that you're trying to be understanding, you need to comprehend how big a deal this is."

"I won't claim to know anything about the genetics involved in addictions running in families. Actually, I don't know much of anything about alcoholism. So maybe you're right. Maybe this is something I'm not equipped to handle."

His gut clenched. "I didn't say this is your—"

"Shhh. Listen. I'm saying I don't have enough information to make a decision, and it seems to me this affects both of us. So I should have a say in deciding something so huge."

He searched for a rebuttal…except what she said made sense, damn good sense. "What did you have in mind?"

"Let's go to an Al-Anon meeting together, let me see for myself what I'm in for. I'll go as a friend if the idea of thinking about forever totally freaks you out."

He fell even more in love with this amazing woman, wise beyond her years and deserving of the absolute best. "We've been naked together. I think we've gone past friendship."

"Can't we be both?"

At a crossroads, they would have to be both—or nothing at all. But then he'd pretty much already figured that one out for himself.

"There's a support meeting tomorrow night."

Make or break time. He'd seen plenty of families and marriages saved by Al-Anon, but most of those people had a foundation before the troubles hit. He and Nikki were starting out with the baggage. He couldn't dodge the dark-cloud feeling that the night would only accomplish one thing.

Helping her walk away for good.

As a trio of C-17s roared overhead for a night takeoff, Nikki stepped from Carson's truck into the parking lot outside the base chapel housing tonight's support group meeting. She hadn't expected the gathering to take place on base, and a smaller group promised less anonymity. Apparently Carson was cool with that.

They weaved around cars and other stragglers making their way toward the entrance, faces shadowy in the dim glow of the overhead halogen lamps. There was so much riding on this night and her nerves were wobblier than the funky heels she'd bought with the intent purpose of making Carson swallow his tongue.

Mission accomplished in that arena, at least.

He slid an arm around her waist as if he expected her to sprint before they reached the looming double doors of the social hall. "If you want to leave at any time, just say the word and we're out of here."

"You've said that twice already. Once when you picked me up, and again at dinner."

And dinner had been so sweet, a back corner table with candlelight and hand holding. He was trying so hard.

Or saying goodbye with a last supper.

"Nikki, I mean it. You don't have to do this."

Stopping by the front sign, she spun on her new heels with an old spunk that she refused to lose now. "Do you even want this to work? Or are you hoping walking in there will discourage me? You've talked about the genetics involved in patterns repeating themselves. Well you decided to break that cycle and sober up. Do you know how freaking outstanding that is? I think it's tough and heroic."

Shaking his head, he swiped aside her hair blowing in her face. "You're seeing things in me that don't exist."

She blocked his hand. "Stop that condescending BS. I'm seeing things in you that you've never allowed yourself to see. You even tried to hide them from me, but I said *heroic* and I meant it."

Was he subconsciously trying to sabotage this before they even made it through the door? And why? She touched his elbow. "Are you going to walk with me into that meeting, or do I go by myself? Because like it or not, I'm involved with an alcoholic."

"Believe me—" his jaw went tight "—I understand that well or we wouldn't be here. I just don't want you to get your hopes up for some magic pill answer tonight."

"There you go with the fatalism again." She couldn't stop the irritation from seeping into her voice when she knew this wasn't the time or place. Backing up the steps, she held up a hand. She refused to cry. "Hold on. I don't want to fight with you before we even get started. Just…just let me freshen up."

And pull herself together.

She spun away and shoved through the front double doors, head ducked as she made tracks past people to the restroom,

Carson's stark, resolved face imprinted in her mind, his oh-so-calm, logical—depressing—tone echoing. He almost sounded like Billy Wade Watkins, always expecting the worst.

Wait.

She gripped the edge of the sink, staring at her face paler than the white porcelain in her grip. Carson sounded like the child of an alcoholic, who'd numbed himself to expecting good things because then nobody could let him down.

Ohmigod. Why hadn't she seen the pattern before?

Because she hadn't been objective—like a teacher—when it came to Carson. Instead of picking a fight with him, she needed to hold firm and simply show him through her stead-fast actions. He was right in saying she'd been unrealistic to expect everything to settle out because of one meeting.

A toilet flushed, announcing an end to her solitary haven. She smiled in the mirror at the stranger stepping from the stall. Resolute and ready to find Carson, Nikki yanked open the bathroom door and into the now-packed entryway.

So much for a small gathering. Where had all of these people come from? And why did so many of them look famil-iar?

Billy Wade—along with his father. She hadn't realized the teen's father was getting help for his drinking, and gam-bling, too, apparently. Vic Jansen stood at their side in what seemed like a supportive role when she hadn't even known Vic had a problem, either. Beyond them, more military acquaintances milled around.

Had each of them been told to put on their perfect face when on base, as well?

She'd been so judgmental of her home life problems growing up, never once realizing all the other military families in pain…drinking, gambling, even some parents supporting teenagers kicking a drug habit.

How many times had she told her students she wasn't looking for perfection, just their best effort? Something Carson needed to hear, as well, for both of them, because there would be no perfect reactions to all of this.

Just a very human, fallible best effort.

She retraced her steps through the lobby looking for him so they could enter the meeting together. She shouldered through, searching. She peeked into the gathering area, rows of folding chairs and a refreshments table, but no sign of Carson.

Maybe he'd gone outside to take a cell call. She stepped through the double doors into the parking lot, her heels crunching on gravel as she pivoted to look…

She bumped against someone, a hard-bodied guy. "Carson?"

A hand clamped on her arm, steadying her as she came face-to-face with…*Kevin Avery?* His cologne stung her nose, his blond hair glinting under the street lamp. "What are you doing here?"

Her question slammed around inside her brain, words spoken now and echoed in her mind from a night nearly three weeks ago.

His grip bit into her flesh. "I've been looking for you."

The ground spun under her feet, memories ricocheting around inside her head. Memories of *him,* a man she'd once dated because he resembled Carson.

She opened her mouth to scream, but he cut the shriek short

with a hand clamped against her lips. Hard. Unrelenting. And horrifyingly familiar. She struggled, wrenching to the side, kicking out.

Releasing her arm, his hand swung down. A dull pain crashed through the base of her skull, once, twice. The edges of the parking lot fuzzed, narrowing along with consciousness. Her dream-vision of the night Gary died now made total sense as she remembered…

Kevin Avery standing over Gary Owens's dead body.

Where was Nikki?

Carson peered over the crush in the corridor for the second time, having already checked the social hall. He'd only turned away for a minute to talk to Vic, and now he couldn't find her. He'd even sent someone into the restroom to look for her. She couldn't have left after she'd been so emphatic about staying.

Damn. Damn. Damn it all, he didn't like this one bit. Where was she and how could someone have plucked her from a group this large?

He didn't like the itchy premonition scratching along the back of his neck. They were in a public place, for God's sake. He pushed through the crowd, making his way toward the double doors.

Stuffiness and noise of the packed social hall gave way to the crisp night air and silence, no sounds other than the occasional whoosh of a passing car. Unease kinking tighter, he scanned the packed lot of empty vehicles all the way to his truck parked at the end with someone inside.

He exhaled a long stream of relief into the freezing night.

Through the back window, he could see Nikki's outline. A stab of disappointment followed.

She'd already given up?

As quickly as the thought slithered into his head, he nixed it, making his way across the dormant lawn toward his Ford. He'd always been the one to walk away, not her. She'd taken a lot of grief from him in the past and still she'd given him another chance. A chance he didn't deserve in any universe.

If she was in the car, then something must have happened to upset her or she wasn't feeling well. Either way, he needed to quit thinking about himself and get over there.

She was right. He'd given up on the two of them before giving them a decent chance. He'd thanked her for trusting him, but what about returning the emotion?

He'd been let down by his parents so many times, let down by adults who should have been there for a kid, somewhere along the way he had stopped putting faith in anyone when it came to relationships. Sure he was a delegation kind of guy at work, but there were tangible gauges of levels of success.

No score guides existed when it came to this whole love gig. He'd told himself he loved her, but hadn't done a thing right in committing. In order for this to work—and hell yes, he wanted Nikki, forever—then he needed to start giving one hundred percent.

He slid into the driver's side behind the wheel, but Nikki kept her face turned to look out. Damn. He had some major backpedaling to do.

"Nikki, listen, I'm sorry about earlier." He stroked up her arm to cup her neck. Was she asleep?

She sagged limply against the seat belt. Strangely slack, not even startling at his touch.

The premonition blasted into full scale alert a second before a looming form rose from the backseat of his extended cab. Carson jerked, ready to launch, attack.

A gun pressed to his forehead stopped him cold. Avery at the other end stopped him colder.

"Major, I'm really sorry it's come to this, but Nikki's enjoying a little nap from a tap on the head." The traitorous lieutenant shifted the gun ever so slightly until it pointed at unconscious Nikki. "Drive, or I'll be having a piece of her while you watch."

Chapter 16

No strange room or temporary amnesia this time. Even through the pounding in her head, Nikki recognized Carson's scent and the sound of his well-tuned truck.

And another cologne. Cloying. Hideously familiar.

The rest mushroomed back to life in her brain. Kevin. In the parking lot. Her mind blazed with thoughts of the night Gary died...then everything went dark.

Did Carson know? Had Kevin somehow stolen the truck?

She started to open her eyes—then rethought. For the moment she would stay limp against the shoulder harness anchoring her to the heated seats until she figured out what was going on.

"Avery—" Carson's voice rumbled from beside her on the driver's side "—you really don't want to do this."

Just the sound of him filled her with love—and dread that

he should be here at all. She'd prayed he was safe back at the church, searching for her, alerting the cops.

Anywhere but here.

"Nikki didn't leave me any choice," Kevin answered from behind her. "She kept digging for the memories."

"You killed Owens?" The shock in Carson's voice echoed within her. Kevin and Gary were friends. Kevin seemed so clean-cut and honorable. Except hadn't she just realized— how long since she'd been at the support meeting?—that military people had flaws and bad apples like anywhere else. Like the police force or other professions that as a whole pledged to protect.

But ohmigod, this went beyond a simple problem.

"Well, Major, I bet on a few games every once and a while to pay off my college loans. A top-notch education is important for getting ahead. You should understand that since your family could afford the best."

Kevin's hot breath blasted against her hair as he moved closer to her. Did he have a gun? He must, or Carson would have taken him out.

The truck shifted into a turn. "A Chief of Staff doesn't have a gambling addiction and bash in people's skulls."

Leather behind her creaked. "A Chief of Staff definitely doesn't have the taint of a gambling addiction on his record—" Kevin's words tumbled faster, angry "—and Owens was going to out me, just because he didn't like my little sideline of taking bets to pay my college loans faster."

"You were a bookie?"

It was all Nikki could do not to blurt her surprise, as well. Good God, how did he expect to keep that a secret? The guy really was an idiot—or so deep in his addiction he'd lost all sense of reason.

"Owens was going to rat me out, something about loyalty to the program. Jesus, all I did was help a few of his buddies in the program make a little extra at the racetrack."

Avery had targeted Gambler's Anonymous members? The guy truly was lower than slime. For money or his addiction or ambition, he'd sold his soul and bartered a few more along with it.

"I couldn't let that happen." His tenor tones pitched higher, faster. High-strung and nervous could be an advantage if they caught him unaware, or a liability if he got twitchy. "I had everything planned perfectly for Nikki to take the fall for an accidental death, self-defense during a rape attempt. Even drugged up, she fought a little when I took her clothes off after Owens was dead. But that just helped set the scene even better."

It took everything inside her to stifle down a shudder of revulsion at Kevin's hands on her while she was helpless. Her cheek even ached with the phantom memory of being slapped. Carson's low growl, however, vibrated the seat.

Kevin's forearm slid around her neck, against her throat. "The Rohypnol I put in her drink should have made her forget everything, but almost right away word spreads around the squadron that she was getting some of her memory back. She must not have drunk enough of the Rohypnol or she has some funky body chemistry. Regardless, I couldn't risk her remembering. I'd hoped the fall from her balcony would look like suicide from the stress."

"You tried to kill her?"

Nikki stifled her gasp of relief that Gary hadn't been un-trustworthy after all, a fact she would savor later, but for now she needed to listen. And while she couldn't think of any log-ical reason for Kevin to spill all—beyond egotistical gloat-ing before he killed them—she appreciated the bit of peace his words brought.

"I had the whole thing planned. I even sent her the fake e-mail from Gary to meet at Beachcombers. I sent one to Gary, too, with a half hour later arrival so I would have time to take care of her drink without him hovering over her like a lovesick nimrod. Thanks to that supersexy note, he really thought she wanted to get a VOQ room for a night together, and of course she was too drugged up to tell him otherwise. I'm so damn smart I even sent the e-mails from a base com-puter and the school library where Nikki tutors so they wouldn't be traceable back to me."

No wonder Reis had been checking out the high school.

Each of Carson's overly deliberate, controlled exhales filled the cab. "If you wanted her dead, why slash her tires?"

"That wasn't me. The way I hear it from Will, that kid of his really did have a crush on her. He would do anything to get her attention."

"Dude, you can't just shoot us."

Could Carson know she was awake and be filtering info? How could he know when she didn't dare give the least hint for fear Kevin would see?

Her heart squeezed at the notion that Carson was as in tune to her as she was to him. She'd longed for that connection and refused to lose it. They weren't dead yet, and damn it, she *did* intend to fight for her man. Whatever it took.

"Like I said, you haven't left me any choice but to kill you. But I'm more creative than that…. Pull over."

She peeked to orient herself and recognized the spot well—the small battlefield where they'd parked, talked. Made love. Water shooshed along the shore with none of its usual soothing tune. Why had Kevin chosen this location?

"Yeah, I followed you two here, and once I could tell you were nice and settled into the back of the truck for a romantic evening under stars, I headed over to your boat. Easy enough to file away at a couple of lines. Too bad you lived. But this time, my plan is foolproof. Brilliant in fact. Worthy of a guy on the fast track."

A rustle sounded from the back, like a paper bag.

"Just a little of this on the seat and even more in your system will explain why you drove the truck off the bridge while coming out to your favorite spot for a little romance."

A little of what?

The splash on her clothes hit an instant before the pungent fumes.

The unmistakable smell of alcohol.

The smell of alcohol saturated the air.

Soaked his senses.

Carson wiped his mind clear of everything but Avery's face and watched for the right time to move. He couldn't let himself think of Nikki slumped and faking unconscious next to him. He definitely couldn't think of the lush harbor side park beyond his windshield. The secluded locale was too full of distracting memories of being with Nikki and how much they had to lose at the hands of this unbalanced megalomaniac.

Megalomaniac. Another five-dollar word to share with Nikki's student, and by God, Carson intended to live long enough to do just that.

His 9mm shifting to kiss Nikki's temple again, Avery passed the bottle of tequila toward Carson, glass glinting in the hazy glow from the dash. "Take it. I even left the worm in the bottle for ya, Major."

Carson closed his fingers around the glass neck, all the while envisioning it was Avery's scrawny throat. Not at all tempted to do anything more than snap it in two and let the amber poison pour away. But he couldn't do that, not yet when he needed to play along for a while more. "Your plan doesn't sound foolproof to me. In fact I can already see a dozen holes."

Talk, you bastard. That would offer up more time to think.

Avery reached behind him again—Carson tensed—and came back with a big buckle belt, which he dropped on the seat. "Owens's. I'm so damn smart I saved this as a contingency in case I needed to set up someone else for the murder." The leather belt thudded to rest beside Nikki. "You never did have faith in my intelligence or ability to lead."

Good God, the kid was a second lieutenant, not the boss. "Then how about you explain your genius to a slower dude like me."

"It's quite simple actually. I'll knock you both out, drive the truck off the bridge and swim away while you drown. The bumps on your head will be attributed to the accident, another tragic DUI."

Well hell, the plan actually sounded as if it could work. His fist clenched tighter around the bottle as he fought off the possibility of losing this battle, ironically fought on a small, nearly forgotten historic field. The whispers of past wars rode the tide's ebb and flow. "Lieutenant—"

"Don't try ordering me around. Not now." Avery grasped a fistful of Nikki's hair and yanked.

She yelped.

Awake.

Damn, he'd thought she might be, but prayed she could simply sleep through this hell.

She blinked, not in the least groggy, apparently having listened to the whole exchange. "Carson, don't do it."

Avery tugged her hair tighter until the skin around her eyes pulled taut. "It's just a drink to save Nikki some pain and ease your own."

"He's going to kill us no matter what." Nikki's unwavering voice held a calm he wouldn't have expected from even a seasoned vet. "You don't have to do this for me."

He understood well what was going on here. There was no reasoning with this monster, only fighting to the death. Being captive had been bad enough with his crew, but seeing Nikki die and being unable to save her was beyond anything he could bear.

And even in the middle of the lowest point in his life, the heavy bottle in his hand didn't tempt him in the least. His mind was clear and focused on what mattered most. *Nikki.*

"I can make it painless for her. I really don't want to do this, but I can't sacrifice my whole future." Avery stared him in the eye without once shifting his weapon from Nikki, but Carson was ready to spring the second the man flinched. "Here's the deal. I'll knock you both out so she can drown while she's asleep. Simple. You just have to go along with my plan. But I can also beat the crap out of her and everyone will assume the injuries came from the wreck. What does it matter if you drink now? You're going to die. You might as well check out with one last taste on your tongue. You don't have to fight it anymore."

"Carson." Nikki's quivering voice drew his attention to her. "It's over."

The defeat in her tone pierced clean through him. He looked in her eyes, the neck of the bottle clenched in his hand with such easy familiarity. He expected to see anguish in her expression, even resignation.

Instead, he saw spunk, anger. Determination.

She hadn't given up at all. She was saying out loud what Avery expected to hear. Her eyes, however, were relaying something else entirely.

Carson glanced outside the windshield, no miraculous weapons to be found on the old battlefield, just the rickety bridge and water. He turned back to Nikki and realized they had everything they needed right here. Trust that flowed both ways.

He wasn't sure how, but she would get out of the line of fire long enough for him to take out Avery. If they died at least Avery couldn't hide a gunshot. There would be justice.

And they might well live. In fact, with Nikki by his side, the odds were damn good.

Eyes on hers, the connection between them hummed so tangibly strong he didn't need words. He raised the bottle, slow, as if torn, his hand shaking which kept Avery's rapt attention off Nikki for a few seconds.

Valuable seconds.

Avery's rabid gaze stayed locked, as if he got off on the control. The Lieutenant's ambition and need for power was all too clear.

Carson didn't dare look away from the bastard in the back, but in his peripheral vision, he could see Nikki's right hand sliding down. For the first time he cursed the luxury seats because the motorized controls wouldn't allow her to slam the sucker back quickly and ram Avery.

But her seat back would lower fast if she released the latch and pushed.

Carson could read her intent as clearly as apparently she read his. The move was risky since it might force Avery's gun arm down, but it *would* catch him unaware. Carson would just have to take advantage of that surprise to adjust the aim.

Even as he raised the bottle to his mouth, the fumes stinging his nose, glass kissing him like a familiar lover—a lover who'd betrayed him—never once did the faith in Nikki's eyes fade.

Time to act.

Simultaneously, she slipped down and slammed back the seat. Avery grunted in surprise. Carson swung the bottle at the copilot's face, jacking the gun arm up in reflexive defense. Glass and tequila sprayed the cab. A bullet pierced the roof, a second through the windshield before the weapon clattered to the floorboard. Nikki ducked, grappling for the gun and clearing the way for him to grip Avery's shirtfront.

Ears still ringing from the gunshots, Carson hauled him over the bench seat, slamming the younger man's face into the dash, once, twice, until he sagged. Unconscious. Thank God.

He couldn't waste a second on relief yet, not until he had Avery restrained and in jail. Convicted to a lifetime in Leavenworth would be damn nice, too.

Carson hauled Avery's limp body from the cab, face to the ground by a rusted cannon, hands behind his back in case the prone man regained consciousness. "Nikki, look in the floorboard for boat lines. Get them, please."

The need for vengeance for Nikki—for young Gary Owens, as well—fired hotter. The dead copilot had struggled valiantly to get his life together and this selfish ass had stolen Owens's second chance. Avery's actions could have subjected Nikki to a lifetime in prison. There wasn't a punishment harsh enough for that.

Nikki clambered over the seat, tugging free a length of boat line. She pitched the rope. Looping fast with a skill honed from years on the water, he trussed their down-for-the-count attacker, hands, ankles, securing him to the small cannon. In some distant part of his brain he heard Nikki placing a cell phone call to the cops. With an extra tug to his best sailor's knots, Carson stepped away from Avery and opened his arms to Nikki….

Damn certain he wasn't letting her go this time.

The next day, Nikki twisted the key in her apartment lock, tickled to her toes to have her life, her job, her home back. Her heart, however, was forever given to Carson.

And if she hurried, she would have time to change before he arrived to pick her up for whatever mystery outing he had planned.

How he'd found time to make preparations after the insane

night they'd had with Kevin Avery's arrest, she would never know. After her 911 call, Special Agent Reis had arrived, as well. The procedural intricacies were mind-boggling as the civilian cops debated with the military security police over who would get the first bite at Avery, one of his crimes off base, one on the government installation.

The SPs won. The kidnapping had begun on base after all, and the murder was the larger crime.

Nikki pushed inside her tiny apartment, no longer minding the bare walls she couldn't afford to fill yet. Instead, they represented all the time ahead of her and experiences to collect. Unlike Kevin Avery who would be locked up for life.

What a sad end for someone with so much potential. As a teacher, she couldn't help wondering where things had gone wrong for him. By the same token, she saw so many students with fewer advantages and opportunities who worked their butts off and made their own successes happen—without excuses.

After giving statements, she and Carson had swept away the glass from the cab of the truck and driven home with the windows open to air out the scent of alcohol and those hellish moments of abject fear. She'd called her parents with the details and to explain she was returning to her apartment. *Her* place and reclaimed life.

She slung her backpack up onto the kitchen bar with a hefty overloaded thump of work to accomplish. Hopefully with Carson at her side. Last night a shower together, making love, celebrating life until they both fell into an exhausted slumber had gone a long way toward settling her ravaged nerves.

Unloading her bag from a blessedly full day of teaching—
a wonderfully normal day with her students and a job she
loved—she knew now to cherish everyday life with her new-
found appreciation. She couldn't wait to show Carson her
blueprints for a miniature Viking ship she wanted to build
with her students for an upcoming unit.

She dropped to sit on the bar stool, her plans spread in front
of her. What a long way she'd come in a few short weeks. Her
crush-style visions of Carson had put him·on a pedestal in a
way that would set anyone up for failure. Now she understood
the value of simple dreams and everyday life, the love of a
good, wonderfully human man to build a future with.

Love was a journey, not a destination.

Her doorbell chimed.

It seemed her trip was about to begin before she had a
chance to change from her work clothes into jeans. She raced
across the carpet, peeking through the peephole, blithe acceptance of safety having taken a serious hit lately.

Her eyes filled with Carson still in his flight suit. A smile
split her face and spread through her. Apparently he hadn't even
taken the time to change, either, instead rushing over to see her.

She swung the door wide. "Hey there, flyboy. I missed you
today."

He swept her into his arms for a kiss that sent that smile
singing further through her veins before he pulled away to
ask, "Would you like to go for a ride?"

She'd thought they were headed to her bedroom, but apparently he was sticking to his plan. "Do I need to change?"

Carson cupped her face, unmistakable love shining in his
crystal-clear blue eyes. "You're perfect as is."

"Not hardly." She arched up onto her toes to steal another kiss, a definite perk on this journey. "But thanks."

He extended his hand and she clasped it without hesitation, snagging her purse and locking her apartment before following him to his truck, a new windshield in place along with freshly cleaned seats. The horror of Kevin's attack would be tougher to erase. Thank God they'd made it through together. Her grip on Carson tightened.

Twenty minutes of easy silence and hand holding later, they reached…a marine repair yard? She squinted in the late-afternoon sun through the chain-link fence until she saw—yes—Carson's sailboat suspended in slings. "Wow, they were able to salvage your boat. That's awesome."

"It'll take time before she's seaworthy again, but the hull is intact." He put the vehicle in park and turned to face her. "That boat holds some irreplaceable memories."

A blush burned her cheeks. "Maybe we'll make more memories when it's afloat again."

"No *maybe* about it once we get her back in the water about a month from now." He winked.

She studied the landlocked craft, winging a prayer of thanksgiving the sturdy craft hadn't capsized altogether. "Thanks for bringing me here. Seeing this helped take the edge off what happened."

"Hell." He thumped his forehead. "I never considered you might not want to sail again. Hey, no sweat if this is a problem for you. I can put this puppy on the market before close of business today."

"You would do that for me?"

"It's just a thing," he answered without hesitation.

"I'm not so sure about that." Her mind filled with an image of Carson on his ship whether it was on the water or in the sky. "At the very least it's a piece of who you are, a way to center yourself."

"I've found a new center."

This moment had been so very much worth waiting for. "Carson, I don't have a problem with sailing. I'm not that faint of heart."

"I never thought you were. You're the strongest person I've ever met." He traced her jaw with callused fingers that rasped so gently against her skin before pointing outside again. "Actually I didn't bring you here just to see the boat. Look closer. I had the shop do one repair right away. See? There. She finally has a name."

Nikki searched, squinted, until she could decipher— "Isis. For my Egyptian project perhaps?"

How fun, Isis finding a flyboy, defying even the constraints of geography and history. A whimsical, romantic notion.

"Most definitely inspired by you and your teaching." He slid his arm along the back of the seat and cupped her shoulder.

"Of course a bit of the legend is backward." She sank against his arm and into spinning out the symbolism of his thoughtful gesture. "Isis saved Osiris from drowning, but you saved me that day in the harbor."

"Honey, you saved me from drowning in ways that have nothing to do with water." He hooked a knuckle on her chin to tip her face toward his. "Knowing you has turned my life around, grounded me, lets me fly, everything at once. The way I remember the story of Isis, she brought Osiris back twice."

"So this is our second chance?"

"If you want it to be." His forehead rested against hers. "I love you, Nikki. I know the words aren't fancy or impressively multisyllabic, but I mean it with everything inside me and look forward to showing you every day for the rest of my life, if you'll let me."

Her arms slid around his broad shoulders only to discover he was shaking as hard as she was. "God, Carson, I've been in love with you for almost three years."

"I'm sorry I wasn't the man I should be then, but I swear to try my damnedest to be worthy of your trust."

"I had some growing up to do myself." How strange to remember at this moment that she'd always told her students perfect wasn't required, only a best effort. Yet, she'd been expecting perfection from her parents, Carson, herself even, and because of that, she'd almost missed out on the purest perfection of all—true love.

His arms tightened. "I don't deserve you."

She arched back to stare him straight in the eyes. "Bull."

"What?

She flicked the zipper tab on his flight suit. "You deserve me and I totally deserve you. Although maybe you'd better not hold me to that when we have an argument, because I'm sure we will sometime since that's a part of loving and living, too." Perfect in its imperfection.

"As long as we get to make up and wake up in each other's arms." A passion she recognized well flamed to life in his blue eyes.

Nikki snuggled closer against his chest again, need sparking to life stronger, hinting it might be time to burn rubber back to her place. "Awaken to desire."

"Always," he whispered the promise against her lips.
Always.
Waking up in his arms.
She liked the sound of that very, very much….

* * * * *

Catherine Mann's Wingmen Warriors *series will continue soon in Silhouette Intimate Moments. But in the meantime, come visit her characters at Silhouette Desire where romance is sure to bloom at Beachcombers. Don't miss Vic's story, available from Desire this April.*

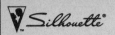

INTIMATE MOMENTS™

Putting out fires...
and setting hearts ablaze!

Firefighter Shelby Fox had a gaping hole
in her memory—and the killer whose face
she couldn't remember wanted her dead.
Detective and longtime friend Clay Jessup
was determined to keep her safe—
and explore the feelings igniting
between them....

Wild Fire
(Silhouette Intimate Moments #1404)

Available February 2006
at your favorite retail outlet.

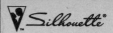

Firefly Glen...
there's nowhere else quite like it.

National bestselling author

KATHLEEN
O'BRIEN

FIREFLY
GLEN

**Featuring the first two novels in
her acclaimed miniseries
FOUR SEASONS IN FIREFLY GLEN**

Two couples, each trying to avoid romance,
find exactly that in this small peaceful
town in the Adirondacks.

Available in February.

**Watch for a new FIREFLY GLEN novel,
Quiet as the Grave—coming in March 2006!**

If you enjoyed what you just read,
then we've got an offer you can't resist!

Take 2 bestselling love stories FREE!

Plus get a FREE surprise gift!

Clip this page and mail it to Silhouette Reader Service™

IN U.S.A.
3010 Walden Ave.
P.O. Box 1867
Buffalo, N.Y. 14240-1867

IN CANADA
P.O. Box 609
Fort Erie, Ontario
L2A 5X3

YES! Please send me 2 free Silhouette Intimate Moments® novels and my free surprise gift. After receiving them, if I don't wish to receive anymore, I can return the shipping statement marked cancel. If I don't cancel, I will receive 4 brand-new novels every month, before they're available in stores! In the U.S.A., bill me at the bargain price of $4.24 plus 25¢ shipping and handling per book and applicable sales tax, if any*. In Canada, bill me at the bargain price of $4.99 plus 25¢ shipping and handling per book and applicable taxes**. That's the complete price and a savings of at least 10% off the cover prices—what a great deal! I understand that accepting the 2 free books and gift places me under no obligation ever to buy any books. I can always return a shipment and cancel at any time. Even if I never buy another book from Silhouette, the 2 free books and gift are mine to keep forever.

240 SDN D7ZD
340 SDN D7ZP

Name	(PLEASE PRINT)
Address	Apt.#
City	State/Prov.	Zip/Postal Code

Not valid to current Silhouette Intimate Moments® subscribers.

Want to try two free books from another series?
Call 1-800-873-8635 or visit www.morefreebooks.com.

* Terms and prices subject to change without notice. Sales tax applicable in N.Y.
** Canadian residents will be charged applicable provincial taxes and GST.
  All orders subject to approval. Offer limited to one per household.
  ® and ™ are trademarks owned and used by the trademark owner and/or its licensee.

INMOM05   ©2005 Harlequin Enterprises Limited

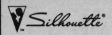

INTIMATE MOMENTS™

Feel the heat with

Fiona Brand's

newest novel of sexy romantic suspense....

With ex-ex-ex-boyfriend Carter Rawlings
back from the military on R & R,
Dani Marlow doesn't want to be just
another benefit of home-leave. Yet when
arsonists threaten her farm, Dani is shocked
into realizing that Carter's presence brings
both the promise of rescue and the new
danger of resurrected emotions.

High-Stakes Bride

(Silhouette Intimate Moments #1403)

*Available February 2006
at your favorite retail outlet.*

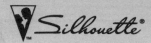

COMING NEXT MONTH

INTIMATE MOMENTS